Zap Dragon
An Adventure Story

Jennifer M Zeiger

Illustrated

by

Esther Rohman

Published by Jennifer M Zeiger of Zeiger Adventure Publishing (ZAP)

Edited by Darren Thornberry

Printed by IngramSpark

First Edition: July 25, 2023

Cover Design by Justin Allen

Illustrated by Esther Rohman

ISBN   978-1-7351226-5-6

jenniferzeiger.com
jennifer.m.zeiger@gmail.com

Esther

Thank you for helping me see the world
through an artist's eyes.

Attention

This book is not intended for you to read straight through! Heaven knows, it'll make no sense if you do.

Instead, read until the book gives you a choice on what to do and then follow the directions to see what happens. Some decisions will lead to success and fame, and others, my dear reader, may lead to misfortune or even death.

Choose wisely for there be strange creatures within these seemingly innocent pages.

Best of luck!

P.S. This book happens to be a spin-off from one of the endings in the *Discarded Dragons* adventure. It can be enjoyed without reading *Discarded Dragons*, but starting with the previous adventure will give you a fuller experience.

Beyond the dumpster's shadow where you hide, the cobblestones are littered with debris from the recent skirmish between a dozen metal dragons and three grimy street boys. The boys push and shove each other at the end of the alley, irritated they lost their treasure trove of finely crafted, if damaged, dragons to a small girl. You watch them, trying to come to terms with your new lot in life.

The Maker's shop where you were made is closed to you now. You've hidden in his discard heap for months, staying away from dragon and human alike ever since he found the defect in your design. But this morning he disposed of the entire heap, his heavy leather gloves protecting him from sharp-edged metal, flaky red rust, and dragon defects combined.

The young girl with her shock baton who just saved the other dragons is now gone. You'd wanted to skitter after her but caution for her safety kept you huddled behind the dumpster. Despite their defects, the other dragons are harmless to handle. The Siren's scream only flattens other dragons and the flame-throated creatures could choose *when* to use their fire.

The same cannot be said for yourself,

however. A mere touch could send the poor girl flying into the wall, much like her shock baton, and you have no control over when it happens. So, although she might *want* to fix your singed marble eyes and rust-covered wings, it would not be *safe* for her to even try.

One of the boys kicks a spring out of his way. His shoe scuffs against the stones. He and his companions start picking through the leftover bits and pieces of debris, drawing nearer. You shrink farther behind the dumpster. If they find you, they'll dismantle you to sell for parts. That is, if they don't smash you in frustration after finding out about your defect.

"Why'd you hold me back?" one asks.

"We were drawing attention," another answers. "Check the dumpster for anything left."

You cower, shivering, and wish again that it'd been safe to scurry after the other dragons and the girl.

Something thuds in the metal dumpster and then a scrap of leather flutters to the stained cobblestones.

"There's nothing here worth selling," the boy grumbles.

A chunk of metal, a bent claw for a larger dragon, pings against the wall and then skips past you under the dumpster.

"Check beneath it. Sometimes stuff falls out."

That's exactly what happened to you

when the Maker tossed you. You hit the edge of the dumpster and, instead of falling into it like the others, you fell onto the cobblestones behind the bin.

Your claws clench of their own accord, screeching against the dumpster's steel as they dig into the side. The sound's lost in the thuds of the boy climbing out but you won't remain hidden for long.

The knees of a boy appear as he crouches to peek beneath. Panicked, you release the dumpster and scurry out the far side, heading for a sewer grate near the end of the alley.

"Hey!" a boy yells, and a moment later there's a tug at your tail.

Instantly, a familiar buzz shoots out from your chest. It rushes along the steel of your body all the way down to the fingers that are starting to lift you off the cobblestones.

Zap!

There's a strangled scream and you're dropped back onto the ground.

"Sorry," you cringe, still racing for the grate.

The taller boy jumps, landing in your way before you can dive to freedom and safety. He holds a burlap sack, intending to catch you.

Your first inclination is to whip the boy in the ankle with your long tail and make a dash for the grate. But, now that you're closer to the sewer, you're not sure if you'll fit through the bars as you're almost the size of a horned owl. And, since the Maker practically finished your design before finding your glitch, you have fully functioning, but thick, metal wings.

Frantic, you cast around for options. You could make a stand to scare them off instead. Now that you've shocked one of them, the boys are eyeing you with far more caution, but with three of them, it'd be tricky. A flash of gray catches your eye. It's an articulated iron spine, crunched in the middle and rusted, but it would give you a longer whip that would conduct your electricity even better than your steel tail.

In your quick search, you also notice a wooden shipping crate against the wall to your left. You've never flown before but with a running start off the crate, you might be able to launch yourself into the air to fly away.

If you whip your tail to escape, go to page 13
If you take a stand, go to page 19
If you attempt to fly, go to page 27

Zap Dragon

There's a scuffing behind you and you look to find the third boy helping the one you shocked get to his feet. It won't be long until you're facing three instead of one again. Although the extra length from the iron spine might intimidate them, you doubt you can win a standoff.

When you look back to the boy blocking your escape, he's stepped closer with his sack, cutting off your route to the shipping crate you considered for flying. *Sewer escape it is*, you think. It's now or never.

Still, you cringe as you whip your body around. Your long tail cracks softly with your momentum. The boy jumps but not fast enough as the tip of your tail smacks into his ankle. It perfectly hits the gap of skin between his ratty shoe and frayed pant leg.

At the same time, a buzz ignites in your chest. It flashes along your metal plates, down the links in your tail, and zaps out the end.

The boy jerks, stumbles backward a few steps, and catches himself on the wall.

It's enough. You dart for the storm drain, your claws scraping on the stones. There's a tug at your hind paw and again your chest buzzes. This time, however, it fizzles. Your defect's like that. Sometimes it shocks with everything in your metal body. Sometimes it fizzles with a soft *pop* that barely leaves a tingle in your limbs.

The boy still jerks away and lets go. You dive for the sewer. At the last moment, you squeeze your eyes closed, expecting to come to a sudden stop when your body wedges between the bars.

Metal scrapes against your chest and wings and along your back, and then you're falling into cool darkness. You open your eyes but only a glimmer of light warns you before you splash into a pool of shallow water below.

Rounded shadows, the heads and shoulders of the boys, appear above. The grate rattles and then you hear, "Stop that! Do you want to draw the beast's attention?"

There's a grumbled response but the shadows disappear.

Darkness, quiet, and a heavy, musty smell surround you. Your sooty marble eyes adjust to the dimness until you make out the dripping walls, a trickle of water along the uneven floor, and the moss growing over everything in a thick mat.

You lay there, listening to the *drip, drip, drip* of water and the occasional rattle of wheels from above. A search with your claws reveals scratches in your metal chest plate but nothing serious.

You roll over to check your wings, testing for damage. Rust flakes away as they open but the long, thin plates expand with a slicing sound like when the Maker sharpens a knife on his whetstone.

Partially extended, you pause, listening. *Drip, drip, drip.* You go back to checking your wings only to pause again.

Drip, drip, skitter, drip.

Out of the darkness, a small creature races toward you. He ducks under your wings and out the far side, never making contact. You glimpse bronze spotted with the mossy texture of oxidization. You're fairly certain it's a rat like those you've seen outside the Maker's shop, except this one's made of metal just like you.

"RUN!" the rat shouts.

Although you've no idea what's chasing him, you don't hesitate. Your wings snap into place against your back and you scurry after the rat, your claws digging into the mossy stones for solid purchase.

The rat slips at a hard corner and slams into the wall. Although you see it, you don't have enough time to avoid slipping on the slimy floor either.

You contort as you slide and smack your shoulder into the wall above the rat without touching him.

In the moment you regain your feet, you catch the glitter of amber eyes from the tunnel behind and a faint shimmer of light on sleek, black metal.

Although you've lived in the Maker's shop your whole life, you know exactly what's chasing you. Every metal creature in the city knows about the elysium wolf. It's an automaton (mechanical creature) like you, but something went horribly wrong in its design. Now it roams the city—including the sewers, apparently—hunting other automatons for the gem-hearts that grant them life.

Panic sends you speeding again after the rat. Your defect might protect you once or twice, but you doubt it'd deter the wolf for long. And eventually it would fizzle and *pop* and that'd be it.

Ahead, the rat vanishes. Before you can process what happened, you run over a large open tunnel that goes straight down. Your stomach drops and, on instinct, you extend your wings.

Since you've lived your whole life in the Maker's shop, you've never flown before. For one brief moment, your wings catch air and there's a wonderful pressure in your shoulder joints, and then your legs hit the ground.

Something brushes your wing. You cringe away but it's too late as the familiar buzz ignites in your chest.

Zap!

The rat screeches and there's a metal

thump against the wall.

A low growl echoes from above.

You can't leave the rat for the wolf but neither can you touch him again. Frantically, you cast around for options. You can't see the wolf above, so he might not have spotted you yet.

To either side the sewer continues.

While you consider which direction to take, you claw huge chunks of moss off the floor until you have pawfuls of the stuff coating your palms. Then, carefully, you pick up the unconscious rat. A large scorch mark mars one of his sides.

There's a gate to the left you can close behind you if you can reach it. It might slow the wolf down but you're not sure for how long as, even from a distance, the gate looks in ill repair. To the right the sewer narrows. If you're fast enough to reach it before the wolf, it might narrow too much for him to follow, but that means you have to be really fast despite carrying an unconscious rat.

With the rodent firmly in hand, you glance left toward the gate and then right toward the narrower tunnel.

If you run toward the gate, go to page 111
If you run down the narrow tunnel, go to page 117

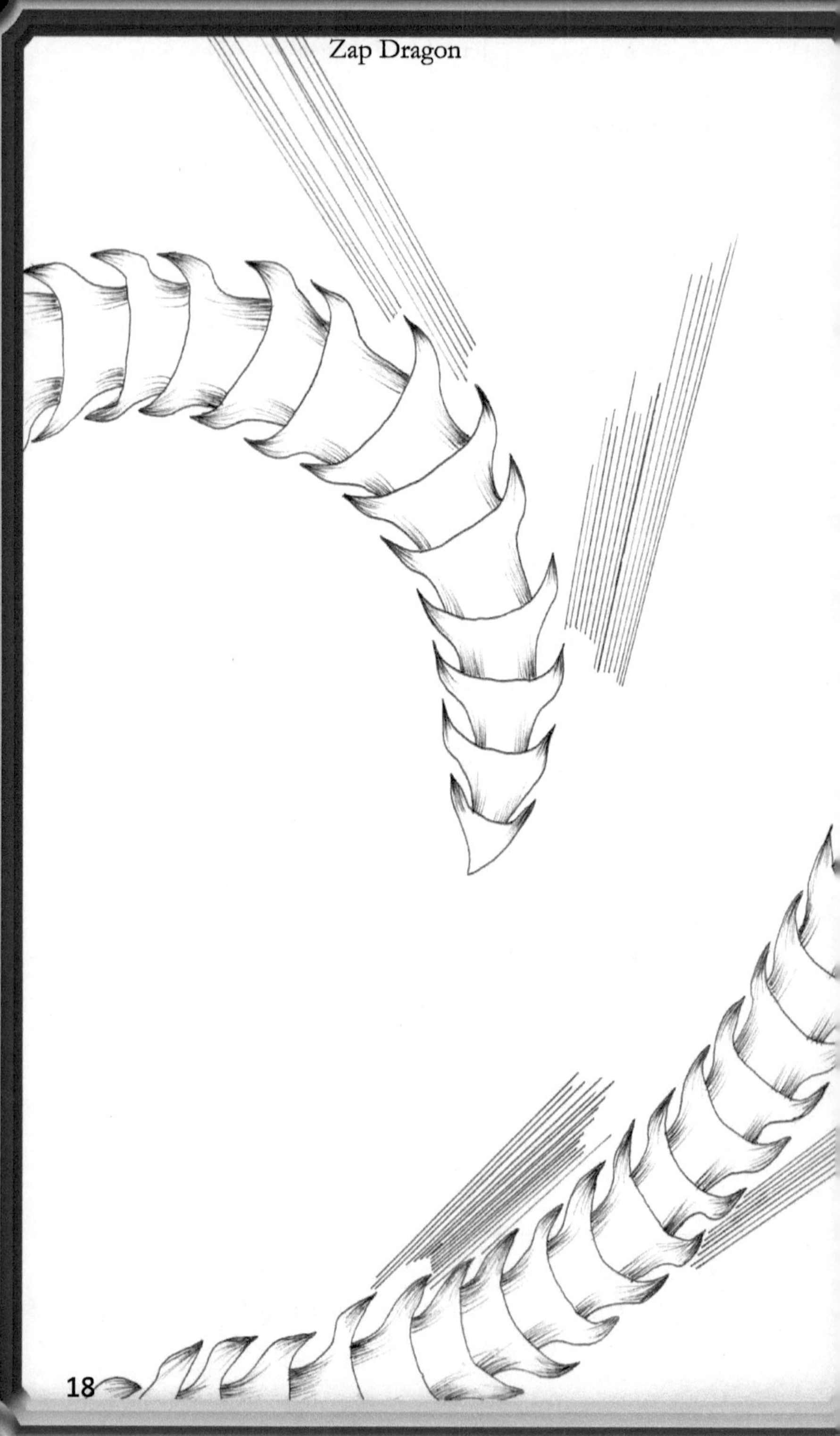

Although your defect shocked the one boy without a problem, it doesn't always work that way. Often it fizzles with a soft *pop* that barely leaves a tingling in your limbs. With your luck, it'll fizzle when you need it the most.

You dive for the damaged spine.

"Hey!" the boy with the sack shouts.

Your paw closes over the iron and you whip it around just as he lunges to close the sack over your head. The spine smacks into his calf. There's a buzz in your chest, but just as you feared, it fizzles with a *pop*. It doesn't matter though. The spine's heavy and the boy flinches away with a howl.

His sack slumps over your shoulder. Shaking it off, you find all three boys staring at you, a new look in their eyes. You can't decide if it's caution or anger. Maybe it's a mix of both.

"Circle it," the taller boy orders.

You retreat a step to put your back against the wall. They can't get behind you but neither can you get past them. Just as you knew would happen, it's now a standoff.

Although there are three of them, you have an advantage. You're not worried about drawing attention whereas the street boys keep casting worried glances toward the end of the alley. If you make enough noise, the boys might run before someone notices. You grip the spine harder and straighten up, extending your wings. The metal screeches, flaking rust, and then the long plates open with a sound similar to a knife on a whetstone.

One of the boys takes a step back. "Never seen one do that before."

"It's still a dumb machine," the tall boy says. "Climb up that ladder and drop a sack over it." He gestures to a wooden ladder farther down the wall.

Your heart sinks. If you'd ever flown before, you'd give it a try now, but living in the Maker's discard heap never gave you the chance.

The boy's feet are two rungs up when he drops back to the cobblestones.

"Got a report," says a new voice from above, "of some boys disturbing the peace." Uniformed men appear at either end of the alley and when you crane your neck upward, you spot a sandy haired man leaning on the top of the ladder. "Round 'em up," the Captain of the City Watch orders.

Your wings snick together as you deflate. The spine drops from your paw with a soft *thunk*. You're about to move off, maybe slide back behind the dumpster where you can consider your next move, when a Watchman reaches for you.

"No. Wait—"

His hand closes

over your shoulder.

Zap!

You're shoved onto your hindquarters. The Watchman flies backward and slams into the far wall.

Of all the times for your defect to go full bore!

Everyone freezes, their surprise clear. The street boy you shocked earlier howls with laughter.

A soft, metallic whine comes from your throat. "Sorry. I'm sorry. I didn't—"

The wooden ladder creaks and you cower even lower when the Captain's boots hit the cobblestones.

The street boy goes silent but the Captain ignores him. "Carson, you okay?"

The shocked Watchman groans. His bright red hair sticks up around his ears and his brows are singed. "Think I just lost five years," he says, "but I'll live."

The tall Captain gestures to another Watchman. "Grab a cage."

A cage? That's worse than the Maker's discard heap. The Watchman disappears and returns a moment later with a wooden cage with metal bars. He flips open the top and asks, "Want me to grab it, Captain Blake?"

The Captain shakes his head while he unclips a pair of thick leather gloves from his belt and pulls them on. "If anyone's getting electrocuted again, it'll be me."

He lifts you into the cage. He doesn't appear angry but neither does he look you in the eyes. You slump against the cage as they head off into the city and wonder what'll happen now.

You're in the city jail. It's not big, just two human cells facing each other and a stack of cages against the back wall between them. The Watchmen let the boys go after a severe warning. You, on the other hand, they brought back and dumped on top of the stack of empty cages. Now you sit watching two of the men play cards.

If you stretched your tail through the bars of your cage, you might be able to touch one of the human cells, but what would be the point? You lay in your cage and huff. You also consider opening the cage with your tail, but again, what would be the point?

The cell to your right is empty, the door slightly ajar.

The cell across from it holds a disheveled man. You can't tell if he's asleep or watching the room from beneath the hat draped over his eyes. His legs are stretched out on his cot and his hands are folded over his lean belly, but he's also propped up against the wall.

Asleep or awake, he's the roughest character you've ever seen, and that includes the street boys who were caked in dirt. A thick, dark beard hides his mouth and the sole of one boot gapes, showing a gray sock and a dirty toe inside.

"Maybe Captain'll take it to Crazy Maze." The men have been discussing your fate for the last hour.

From what you can tell, Crazy Maze is an artisan who lives outside the city due to the explosive nature of his work. The Watch sometimes brings him mechanical creatures they don't know what else to do with since he's apparently good with automatons.

Firm steps sound against the boardwalk a moment before Captain Blake shoves through the door. "Arm up," he commands.

The men hop to, forgetting their cards on the table to grab their rifles.

"What's happening, Captain?"

"The Barrow Gang's headed our way. It's just us three to hold them off until backup arrives."

You catch the glitter of eyes under the other prisoner's hat. He doesn't move but his lips twitch.

You shift in your cage, grasping the bars, and the Captain shoots you a glance. This time, he meets your eyes but it's brief as he loads a rifle and heads toward the front window.

Something sails through the window and starts hissing as it thuds against the wooden floor. Heavy, thick smoke blossoms into the air. On instinct, you stop breathing. Human coughs erupt through the room and the smoke obscures what's happening.

A gun goes off, making your ears ring, and men start shouting. You hear thuds and grunts and imagine the Watchmen fighting the gang.

"Got y'r Captain!" shouts a voice. From its location, it's probably the man in the cell.

A gust of air swirls the smoke, revealing the prisoner holding the Captain by the throat, pinning him against the bars of his cage.

"Don't move err I'll finish 'im."

Stillness descends over the jail. The Captain's eyes are watering, but he still shoots a look your way. Then he flicks his eyes at the cell.

He wants you to zap the bars? But that would shock him too. Or your defect will fizzle and just make the prisoner angry.

The Captain flicks his eyes again, this time urgently as a bandit emerges from the smoke with the cell's keys.

He's close enough you could reach him with a strong jump. You might be able to unlock your cage with your tail and attack him. It'd certainly create a distraction and give the Captain a chance to break free but it's a gamble as you're not sure how fast you can get the lock open.

If you zap the bars, go to page 35

If you create a distraction, go to page 77

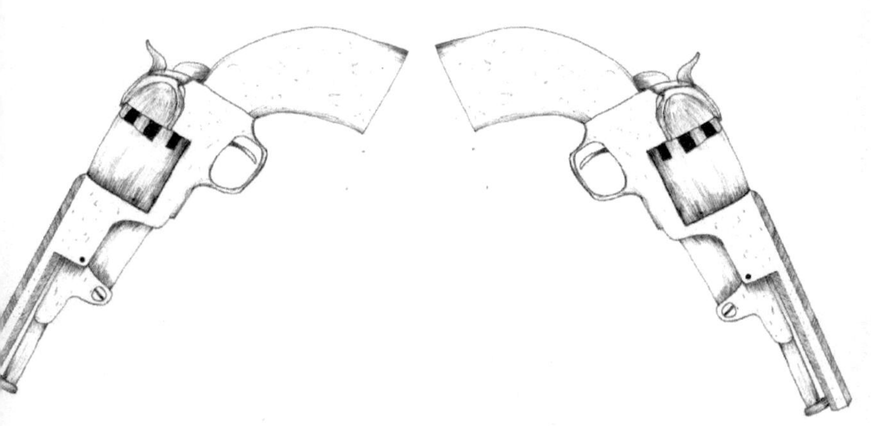

Before the boy can react, you're scampering for the wooden shipping crate as fast as your legs will carry you. You've never flown before, but if you can prevent yourself from zapping another person today, you're willing to try it.

"Dang dragon!" The boy's after you, the scuff of his feet warning that he's far too close for comfort.

You jump for the shipping crate. Since it's too tall for you to make the top in one bound, you smack into the side and sink your claws into the wood about halfway up. The box teeters precariously under your sudden weight. Scrambling upward, you make the top and race for the far side.

The box continues to teeter and you stumble side-to-side but there's no time to back up and try for a smoother takeoff. Already, the boy's reaching to pull the crate over.

Spreading your wings with a sharp snap and the screech of rusted metal, you fling yourself off the side. The boy jumps, his hand reaching, and his fingers brush your legs. You spin and almost collide with the wall before you remember to use your wings. One solid flap, though, and you're past the boy and gliding for the open street beyond the alley.

There's a wonderful pressure along your

chest plates and under your wings. You give another tentative flap and rise higher, basking in the sudden feeling of freedom.

It's amazing and exhilarating and you suddenly understand why the other Discards were so determined to finish their designs. You look back to see the three frustrated boys racing after you before you exit the alley.

They're too slow. You give one more flap and sail out into the open street beyond.

Immediately, a carriage clips your tail and your smooth soar turns into a hazardous spin. People and horses and carriages flash past your snout. You regain control only to have a rider on his horse whoosh by. The air from his passage sends you careening toward the side of the street and the baker's front window.

You have only a second to make a snap decision to bank left and tangle with the powerlines or right and risk coming close to the street boys still following you.

If you go toward the power lines, go to page 31
If you go toward the street boys, go to page 149

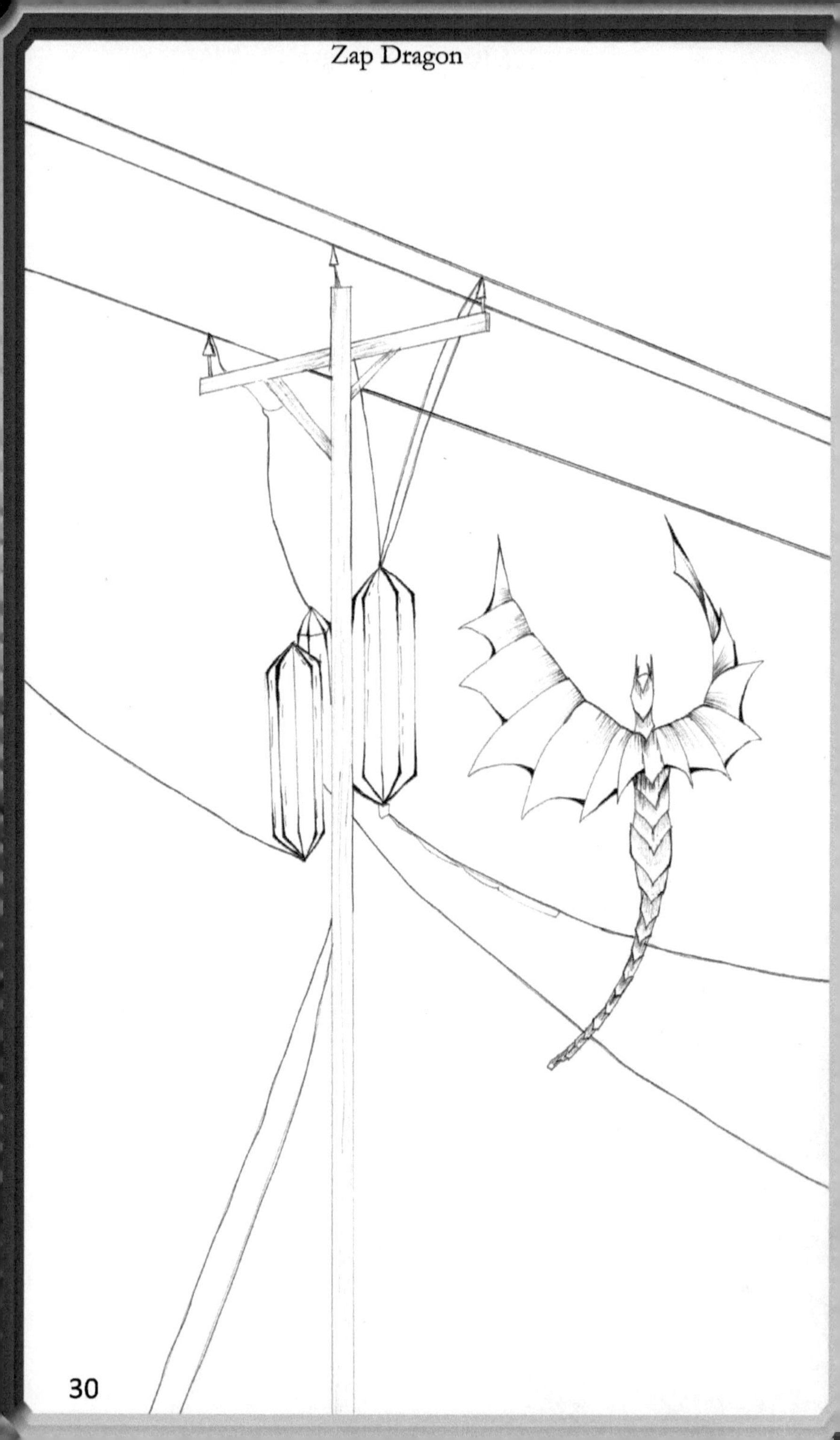

Banking hard to avoid a collision, you turn left and tuck your neck to avoid the thick power lines. You barely miss the cables as you hear them whoosh past. Exhilaration fills your chest like a too deep breath. Suddenly, your wingtip clips the bricks of the bakery's wall and you spin and slam into a power pole instead.

There's a large node on the side of the pole that makes you think of the power-gems the Maker sometimes uses to power dragon wings. Except such power-gems are too powerful and he's never managed to use one without it fusing something together within the dragon.

Right as you think this, the node starts glowing and there's a faint buzz from within it.

ZAP!

You scream, flying backwards. With a thud, you smack into the wooden roof of a passing carriage. Your vision sparks and your gears twitch but you feel the carriage slow and stop.

"Something's hit us, my lady," the driver says.

The carriage opens and a woman's purple hat appears. The driver, a lean man with a weathered face, looks disgruntled as the woman joins him on the driver's seat to peer at you on the roof. At least, you think he's disgruntled. Your vision continues to spark and your gears twitch erratically. The wheels in your jaw shriek when you finally manage to close your mouth.

"The poor thing," the woman says. She reaches for you.

You try to scamper away. All you manage to do is open and close your claws. You realize a wingtip is wedged into the carriage roof and, worse still, the metal plates are stuck open.

The woman's delicate fingers close over the wing, and you wait for everything to go haywire again.

Except nothing happens.

No buzz. No zap. No scream.

"The metal's warm. The poor dragon must have collided with a transformer. Free the wing, Geoffrey. I'd like to see if we can help."

"It's an automaton, Lady Mae, and badly damaged. I doubt there's much we can do."

Lady Mae scowls. "Free the wing," she says again and disappears back inside the carriage.

Geoffrey grumbles but tugs you free. At first, he acts like he's going to toss you onto the carriage seat through the open window but at the last moment he seems to think better of this and politely hands you to Lady Mae.

You're still amazed you're not zapping anyone. You don't move when Lady Mae sets you on the seat across from her. She tries to close one of your wings but it doesn't budge and instead the pressure just slides you across the bench. She frowns, tapping her lips in thought.

"Maybe I should sell you to the dragon artisan. Or maybe Sir Leo's daughter could fix you and I could keep you…" she continues to mutter but your mind sticks on the mention of the artisan. Is that the Maker? He already threw you into the discard heap but that was because you were dangerous. If he can now work on you, would he decide to finish your design? You've no idea but you suddenly find the notion that the Maker could finish you an enticing possibility.

But then Lady Mae's second suggestion takes hold. She might keep you? What if this girl, Sir Leo's daughter, can't fix you? Should you ask her to keep you? Uncertainty turns the gears in your stomach.

Lady Mae continues to contemplate aloud and you realize that, if you don't say something, she's going to take you back to the Maker. You've never known a human who spoke with an automaton before but none of the dragons were allowed to speak in the Maker's shop, so your experience might be skewed. Would it scare Lady Mae if you asked her to keep you?

————————————

If you say something, go to page 89
If you remain silent, go to page 95

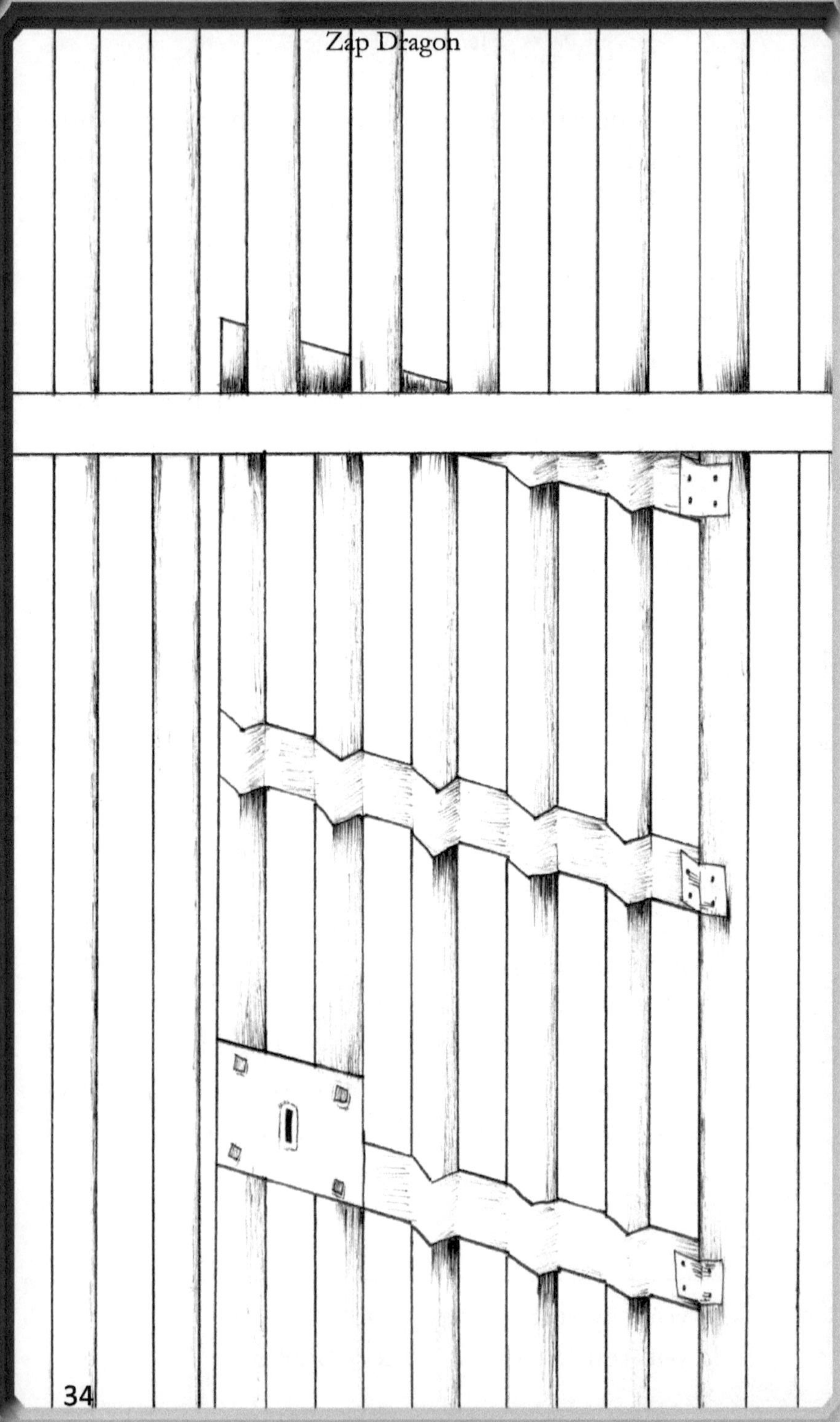

Your claws dig into the wood of the cage floor. This is the first time in your life someone's asked for your help and you can't just watch as the bandits get away. It's a long stretch to the bars of the human cell but you have to try. Shifting to the far side of the cage, you snake your tail through the bars.

No one, except the Captain, notices. You stretch, shuddering with effort, and touch the tip of your tail against the metal.

Captain Blake stiffens, anticipating the shock, but nothing happens. Not even a fizzle in your chest. Twin furrows appear between Captain Blake's brows.

No, no, no, no! You smack the bar this time and it gives a ping like a dropped coin.

Your chest buzzes.

Zap!

You fly across the cage, and it tumbles from the stack to crash against the floor. Surprisingly, it doesn't shatter. It rolls a couple of times and then you find yourself looking at the jail through the top of the cage.

Not far from you, Captain Blake lies unconscious against the door of the unoccupied cell. Just like you, he must have been thrown from the shock.

35

Across from him, the prisoner also slumps unconscious inside his cell. He's draped over the cot like a child's thrown-aside rag doll.

"Lock 'em in and check the boss," a bandit orders.

Your attempt to help only made matters worse! Disappointment turns the gears in your belly as the bandits haul the Captain into the open cell. They shove the other two Watchmen in behind him and then they check on their boss.

"He's alive," one confirms.

"Carry 'im. We need outta here afore the rest of the Watch returns." A bandit throws the big man over his shoulder.

You slump in dismay as they leave.

"Captain?" The Watchman you shocked in the alley, Carson, shakes Captain Blake's shoulder once they're gone.

He groans and relief floods your limbs with a tingling just like when your defect fizzles.

"That automaton about killed you. The useless thing," the other Watchman says as he helps the Captain sit up.

"Least it tried, Parkins," the Captain says. Your chest clenches. With his blond hair singed and eyebrows wild, he looks like he tangled with a power transformer, but instead of the anger you expect, there's gratitude in his eyes.

Determination builds within you. You slide your tail out the top of your cage and curl it around to insert the tip into the lock.

"What's it doing?" Parkins asks.

"Unlocking itself," the Captain says.

There's resistance in the lock. With a gentle sideways pressure, the resistance disappears.

"It can do that?"

The lock clicks and the top of the cage swings open with a push.

"Guess so."

You'd suspected before that you could unlock the cage but what would have been the point? It wasn't like you could go back to the Maker's shop.

But now you have a purpose and it feels good, like spreading your wings and shaking off the rust.

You waddle to the door of the Captain's cell and look up. You're not a small dragon but the lock's still too high to reach from the floor. Grabbing your cage, you haul it over to stand on.

"Don't touch the bars," the Captain warns his men as you turn backward and climb your hind legs up the bars until you're doing a handstand. It's awkward, but it positions you to insert your tail into the cell's larger lock.

The resistance this time is heavier. You grunt with the effort and something pinches just before the lock gives a thud and the resistance disappears. When you pull your tail free, you find the tip squished but the cell door swings open and you shrug off the damage.

"Well, I'll be," Carson says.

"Gather the men," Captain Blake orders. "We can't let the Barrow Gang get too far. Boss Gingham's supposed to stand trial tomorrow."

The Watchmen hustle to do as ordered. Now that you've accomplished your goal, you deflate, staring after them when they leave.

It's a moment before you realize Captain Blake's watching you.

"Can't control it, can you?" he asks.

He's talking to you! This day is full of firsts. You shake your head in answer.

"I can't fix you myself," he says, "but you can come with us to capture the Barrow Gang and we'll mitigate your zapping issue as best we can. I have a feeling you could be a very handy Watchdragon. Or—" he pauses, seeming to debate the wisdom of his words, but then he shrugs and says, "Or I can give you to Crazy Maze. He'll at least make it safe for you to touch things. Your choice."

———————————————

If you help the Watchmen, go to page 41
If you pick Crazy Maze, go to page 59

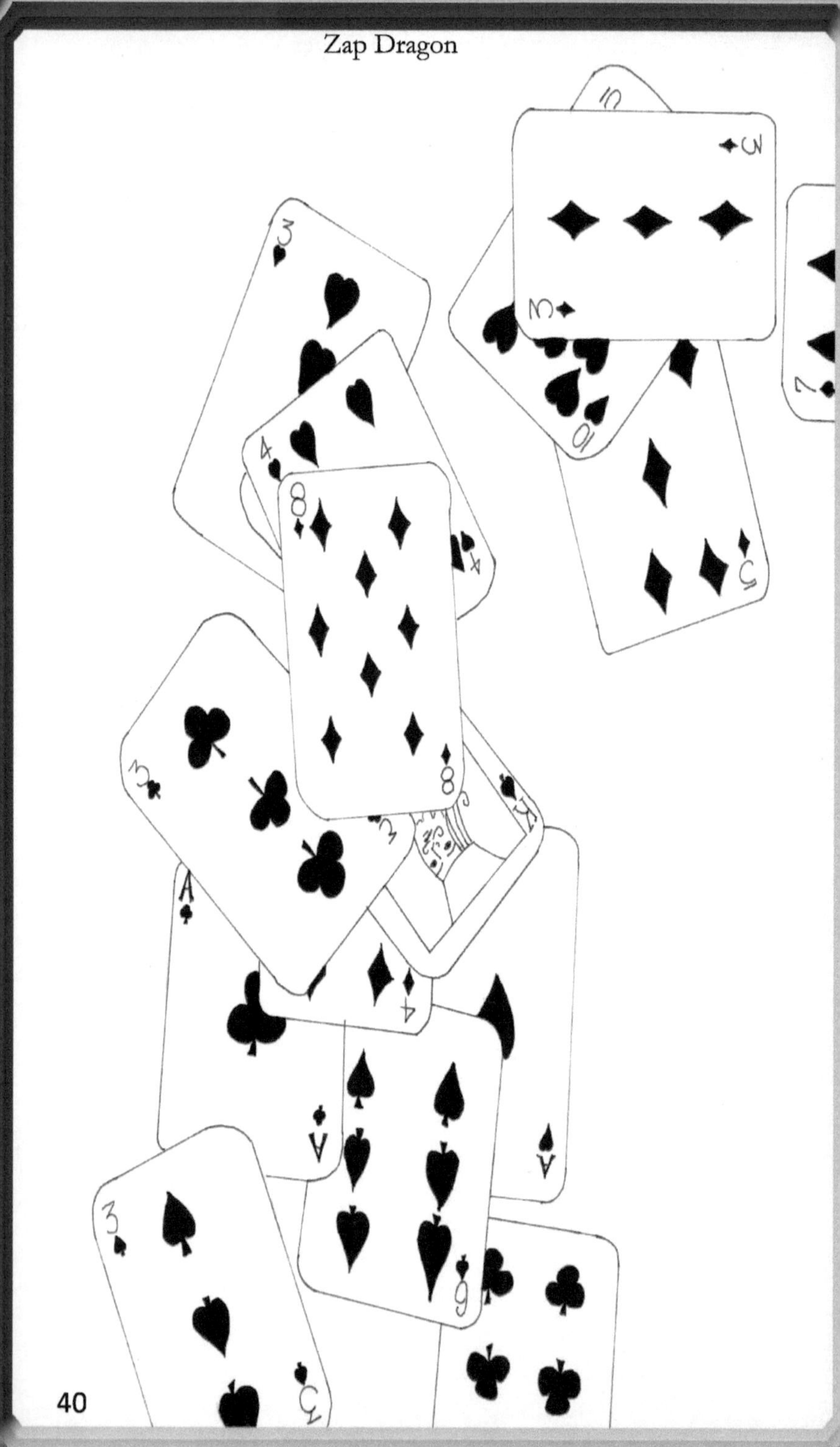

You'd dearly love not worrying every time someone touches you that you're going to zap them across the room, but looking at Captain Blake, you realize he might actually become your friend. After months alone in the discard heap, you can't pass that up.

"I'll help," you say.

Captain Blake grins, pleased. He unclips his leather gloves and lifts you from his desk to the table where the men were playing cards.

"I've a friend who keeps owls. I'll see if we can borrow equipment from him. Stay put."

You don't have to be told twice. With a thump, you sit down on the table. Your nervous energy builds while you wait for him to return. What did you just agree to? Needing something to do, you gather up the cards and start trying to figure out how to shuffle them.

The Captain comes through the door and pauses, eyeing the claws you have wrapped carefully around the cards.

"Not going to light those on fire, are you?" he asks.

You hadn't considered that. "Never zapped paper before," you answer. As far as you can remember, that's true, but then you also don't have a clue what triggers your defect, so you gently set the cards down.

He holds up a strange harness made of

leather. "We're improvising," he says. "This will slide over your tail and up along your chest to help protect me. Between that and this," he gestures at the heavy padding of leather over his right arm and shoulder, "we should be safe if we trigger your zapping issue."

You've never worn a harness. A part of you cringes at the idea but you're not about to balk at the first obstacle. You step forward and Captain Blake pulls the straps under your wings and then ties them over your neck. It reminds you of the heavy apron the Maker sometimes wears.

"Don't extend your wings while I'm carrying you," the Captain cautions with a raised finger. "I don't want to be zapped by a stray wingtip."

"Understood," you say, testing the harness by waddling around the table. Surprisingly, it's snug around your torso and doesn't hinder your movement. You step onto the Captain's arm when he offers it and grip tightly to the thick padding.

"Captain?" Carson the Watchman, peeks through the door. He eyes you but doesn't speak his doubts as he says, "Men are gathered."

"Good. Let's go."

Parkins, the small Watchman who called you useless back at the jail, happens to be an excellent tracker. You're determined to prove his assessment of you wrong.

He led the group on horseback out of the city and into the Merchant Forest. Now he crouches beside the road fingering the leaf of a fern.

"They went that way." He points toward the mountains and into the thick evergreens.

You peer into the woods, finding everything at a distance is blurry. Has it always been that way? You don't know. You've always lived in the Maker's shop, then in the jail. The distances around you now are much greater than anything you've encountered.

"There's a ravine about two hundred meters in that direction," Parkins says. "They probably settled there for the night."

You wonder if the hazy distances are because of the soot covering your eyes. Testing the theory, you lean over and swipe your head sideways across the Captain's glove. When you look up, you gasp, finding the branches on the trees have sharp needles and the distant mountaintops look white. Quickly, you wipe your other eye and blink in happy surprise.

"Is that thing sane?" Parkins asks.

The world's layered in a white sheen from your marble eyes but the ever-present gray tinge is gone. Now the only shadows you see are from the long stretch of trees as the sun sinks below the horizon.

"Sane enough," Captain Blake says. "Let's scout the bandit camp."

"How about we use your dragon?" Parkins asks.

You duck your head, surprised, and then freeze when you almost touch your snout to the Captain's neck.

"They'll be on the lookout for us approaching on foot," Parkins explains, "but a dark shape in the sky won't raise any suspicions, especially as dusk draws closer."

Your claws dig harder into Captain Blake's arm padding. *Flying?*

"What do you say?" the Captain asks you.

Parkins will surely think you're useless if you admit you've never flown before, but then, when he sees you try to take off, he'll know anyway.

"I've never flown," you whisper.

There's a glint of understanding in the Captain's eyes. "Up to you," he says. "Fly over to scout or stay with us and we'll scout on foot."

If you scout alone, go to page 47

If you stay with the group, go to page 53

Jennifer M Zeiger

A small dragon in the Maker's shop used to sneak out at night to find parts. That dragon had never flown before either, but it was bold enough to try. Your stomach gears churn but you straighten to your full height and say, "I'll scout."

"We'll need numbers and the layout of their camp," Captain Blake says.

"Numbers and layout," you repeat.

It occurs to you that if you take off from the Captain's arm, you might clip him with a wing by accident. "Maybe set me on that tree?" You point to a pine branch that overhangs the road.

The Captain maneuvers his horse over and lets you step onto the branch. It dips under your weight and your stomach gears grind harder. Below, the ground seems to move but you know the illusion's caused by the pine branch's swaying. You've never been more than a few feet off the ground despite being a dragon with wings.

"What if it spirals right into their camp?" Parkins asks.

Carson answers, "It'd be a great distraction."

"Hush," Captain Blake says. "Give the dragon a chance."

It's now or never, you think. You spread

your wings, the metal plates flaking rust, and jump.

For a heart-stopping moment, you fall. The image of you smashing into the ground rushes through your head, and then pressure builds against your wings and your fall shifts into a long glide just above the dirt.

A horse whinnies as you fly past. You give a tentative flap and, thrillingly, you soar upward, snaking through the trees until you rise high enough to fly out over the canopy. An expanse of green trees and darkening sky opens before you.

Orienting off the road and the Watchmen below, you angle toward the ravine Parkins mentioned. The faint scent of smoke wafts up from the ground. With the gathering dark, it's not hard to spot the flicker of a tiny cooking fire. At this point, you're too high to see numbers or layout, especially with the trees and gathering gloom.

Tilting your wings instinctively, you glide lower, counting men as they become visible.

One, two, three, fou—

There's a flash of gray and an iron falcon slams into your side. His talons sink into your harness but don't contact your metal as the bird pulls, trying to control your direction.

It never occurred to you that the bandits might have their own mechanical lookout! Your steady flight becomes a tug-of-war as you start to plummet. If you can knock the bird out, you might be able to escape before the bandits notice.

You twist, smacking your tail against the falcon's chest. It's only as you connect that you remember the leather harness covers your tail too. There's no familiar buzz in your chest. No zap. But the impact loosens his hold. You tear away, flapping hard to gain distance.

The falcon screams an echoing, metallic challenge and gives chase.

Frustration builds in your chest. There's no way the men below didn't hear that scream.

You've barely said a handful of words in your life, much less shouted at an opponent, but as you notice the bandits scrambling about below, you want to scream back. Even in the gathering dark, you make out the long barrels of their rifles. They're getting ready to search the forest. They'll find the Captain and his men in minutes.

You spin on the falcon, open your creaking jaws, and roar a challenge back that vibrates your metal plates and echoes through the ravine. The vibration doesn't stop. It builds into a familiar, internal buzzing that starts to rattle the screws of your chest plate.

Just as the pressure grows too strong and you think you're about to explode, you roar again, and a rope of electricity jumps from your open mouth and slams into the falcon's chest.

It leaves a powerful afterimage on your eyes, but you don't miss the sudden sooty starburst coating the falcon's body. Its wings stall mid-flap. It suspends in midair and then plummets.

You dive after it. The ground rushes toward you and you're in the midst of the Watchmen battling it out with the Barrow Gang before you sink your claws into one of the falcon's trailing wings. You'd intended to catch the bird to slow its descent—it might still be alive, after all—but as you flap hard to stall your dive, you notice Boss Gingham about to shoot Parkins in the back.

Spinning, you launch the falcon at Boss Gingham. It clips him in the back of the head and his shot goes wide.

Parkins looks over, startled, and after a pause, salutes you. Then he takes the opportunity to knock Boss Gingham out with the butt of his rifle.

"Boss is down!" he shouts.

Like he pulled the gem-heart out of a dragon, the fight drains from the rest of the gang. Rifles drop to the ground and hands rise into the air.

You land and stumble on wobbly legs. It feels like all your screws are loose.

As the Watchmen tie their prisoners up, Parkins hollers to Captain Blake, "Think we could call it Watchdragon Zap?"

You freeze, casting a look toward the Captain. He winks and says, "Seems to fit. What do you think, Watchdragon?"

The End

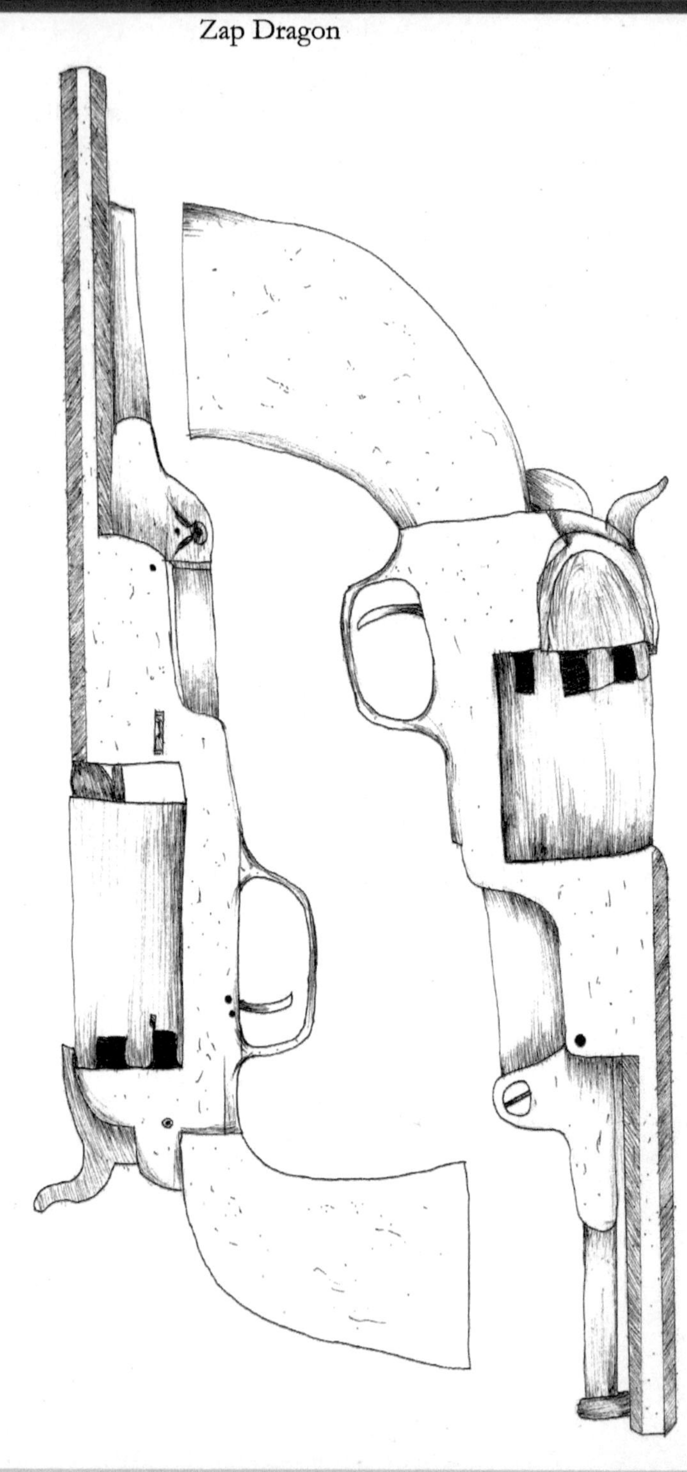

You think of the small dragon in the shop who used to sneak out at night to find parts. That dragon had never flown before either, but it was bold enough to try. On the other hand, it was also that dragon's antics that got the whole discard heap thrown into the dumpster that morning.

"This might not be the best time to test my flying skills," you say.

The Captain nods, a bit disappointed you think, but he looks to Parkins and orders, "Scout ahead."

Parkins shrugs and disappears through the trees. Not long after he reappears and reports, "Six men including Boss Gingham." He crouches down and draws a small circle in the dirt with a stick. "One's cooking here," he indicates a spot with an X, "two are keeping watch here and here," more Xs, "Gingham's laid out napping here and the other two are playing dice here."

The Captain studies the sketch. "Alright, here's the plan."

Moments later, everyone's in position. Captain Blake opted for speed instead of stealth and everyone's still saddled. The plan's simple. Your group of six Watchmen are now arrayed at intervals at the mouth of the ravine. At the Captain's shout, they'll ride in and take the bandits by surprise. If all goes as hoped, the fight should be over before it even begins. Your job is to guard the Captain's back from his shoulder. You're using your sheathed tail wrapped into the back of his leather jacket to secure yourself.

Captain Blake steadies his horse and takes a firmer grip on the reins. "Hold tight," he whispers to you and then gives a carrying shout to his men.

The horse's gait changes and through the trees comes the thud of hooves. You crouch lower, digging your claws harder into the thick padding on the Captain's shoulder. Instinctively, your tail curls farther into the back of his jacket.

A familiar buzz ignites in your chest.

Not now!

You clutch tight, hoping the zap doesn't throw you from your perch or shove the Captain from his horse. The buzz vibrates your screws. You lean your face away from the Captain on the off chance the shock makes you twitch. And then the buzz fizzles with a soft *pop*.

"Watchmen comin'," shouts a bandit. The sharp report of a rifle splits the air and the Captain flinches.

Is he hit? You search and spot a trail of blood across the horse's side. It winged the horse.

Following that trail, your

stomach sinks. The wet trail stops at the Captain's leg. It must have lodged there. Somehow, the Captain ignores the wound despite the blood soaking his pantleg. He raises his pistol.

The sentry who shot him raises his own pistol and takes another shot just as the Captain shoots back. The man drops.

The Captain's horse stumbles. He tries to jump free before the horse goes down, but his injured leg doesn't cooperate and the world tilts sideways. You pull your tail free of his jacket and jump right before the horse pins the Captain to the ground by his leg.

He screams while the animal thrashes. It finally stands and bolts and you realize it must have stumbled instead of getting shot. Captain Blake tries to rise and falls back.

"Caught me a Watch Capt'n," the prisoner from the jail, Boss Gingham, emerges from the trees and aims his long barreled six shooter at Captain Blake.

You pull the strings holding your harness and wrestle out of it, thinking to rush at the man.

"Don't move, creature," Boss Gingham snarls.

You freeze.

You can't make it to the bandit by running at him. He's too far away and with his pistol trained on you, he'll shoot you well before you reach him. Another idea comes to you. You just need a moment of distraction. That's all. Since the Captain still has his heavy leather gloves on, you have a simple, if desperate, plan.

A bandit behind Boss Gingham screams and he looks back to where Carson's wrestling one of his men. They roll into the dishes set out for the bandit's supper and the tin plates clatter to the dirt.

"Throw me," you hiss.

Captain Blake doesn't hesitate. Just as Boss Gingham's turning back, you collide with his chest. Reflexively, he catches you and stumbles. Realization widens his eyes. He tries to pitch you away, but you grab pawfuls of his shirt to hang on. You're not going to get a better chance to zap him but, as you will your defect to work, nothing happens. No buzz. No fizzle. No zap.

Boss Gingham grunts and lets go. You hang awkwardly from his shirt as he points his pistol at the Captain again.

Giving up on your defect, you latch onto his wrist with your long tail and pull.

His shot goes wide. The concussion of it hurts your ears but a familiar buzz ignites inside your chest.

Zap!

Boss Gingham screams. His eyes roll upward and he collapses. At the last moment, you spring away to avoid getting pinned under him and land in a shower of pine needles.

"Gingham's down!" shouts Captain Blake.

Like he pulled the gem-heart out of a dragon, the rest of the gang hesitates, and then their rifles drop to the ground.

You scurry over to check the Captain's leg.

"It's fine," he says.

"It's still bleeding," you say. You cast around for something to staunch the blood and grab your discarded harness. Someone less shocking will have to dig the bullet out later.

As you're tying off the knot, Parkins wanders over with the Captain's horse. "Not sure why you trust that thing, Captain," he says, eyeing you.

"The dragon saved my life twice over, Parkins. Think I'll keep it around."

Parkins shudders and walks away.

Behind his back, the Captain grins. "What do you think?" he asks. "Want to stick around?"

The End

Your tail sways against Captain Blake's back with the horse's gait. He found a blanket to insulate you and is letting you ride on his shoulder as you head toward Crazy Maze's.

You would have loved to be a Watchdragon, but without being able to control your defect, you turned down the offer. It wouldn't be fair to the Watchmen if you're a liability instead of a help.

Captain Blake accepted your decision with a simple nod.

As the city disappears and the Merchant Forest surrounds you in its thick evergreens, your paws shake where you clutch the blanket. The unfamiliar scent of pine and juniper engulfs you and you breathe in the smell of leather coming from the Captain's jacket for comfort. You've never been outside the Maker's shop, much less the city, and the world suddenly seems huge. You feel creaky, like the rust on your steel is grating against the edges of your plates.

"Crazy Maze is weird," the Captain speaks, pulling you from your thoughts. This is the first time he's spoken since you left the jail. "He's not a bad man. Be bold and you should be fine."

The trees open onto a large meadow full of purple, blue, and white wildflowers. A huge stone tower rises directly in the middle. You crane your neck backward farther and farther to take in its height.

"Captain!" greets a deep voice with the distinctly hollow quality of an automaton.

A creature, bottom half lion, top half eagle, with massive silver wings sprouting from its back, wanders around the side of the tower. If you were to guess, you'd say he's made of aluminum. He appears lighter and more agile than the lion's thick body would suggest. The gears at his hips shift smoothly with each step and his wings drape around his sides, leaving thin trails in the wildflowers. You swallow envy at its immaculate condition.

"It's a griffin," Captain Blake whispers. Then, to the creature he says, "Titan, is Maze around?"

The griffin sits and his eyes narrow. They're not gem-eyes like the Maker put in all his dragons, but kaleidoscopes that shift with small circular plates. "Perhaps. Are you bringing him a new project?"

"Titan, let the good Captain's dragon in!" shouts a voice from inside the tower. "He always brings me the best puzzles!"

Your claws dig into Captain Blake's leather jacket.

"Be bold," the Captain

whispers again as the griffin huffs.

Titan smacks a paw against the side of the tower with a resounding thud. His movement reveals a piece of rusted metal sticking out of his paw like he stepped on a tack but then the stones of the tower split open, revealing a doorway and a staircase beyond, and you forget about the griffin's paw.

"I can't go with you," Captain Blake gets down from his horse and lets you off his shoulder. "Good luck."

Luck? Has the Captain never been inside Crazy Maze's? You stare into the maw of the tower as he rides away. It's dark inside and all you can really see are the first three steps and the circular stone wall. You're about to brave the doorway when a mouse scurries out of the woods and stops at your feet. The glistening red metal of its ears reminds you of a female dragon from the Maker's shop.

"Don't go! Follow me!" the mouse scurries away, running a zigzag to avoid Titan's heavy paw as it races back to the trees.

"The nuisance!" Titan grumbles. "He'll have you rusted out within a week." He waves a paw toward the open tower. "Better not keep Maze waiting."

If you enter the tower, go to page 63
If you follow the mouse, go to page 71

Your claws click on the stone steps as you climb into the tower. It's a long way up, but if Crazy Maze can indeed fix you, it will be worth it. At long last, the staircase opens into a circular room that's bigger than the Maker's shop. Towering bookshelves line the walls, broken only by a small kitchen nook and what appears to be a bench just like the Maker's. A subtle smell, like vanilla and wood, surrounds you and you wonder if it's from all the books.

A lean mechanical cat with purple eyes grooms her tail on one of the shelves. The cotton cloth she's using brings out a golden shine to her metal. She looks up with an amused expression when you step into the room.

Your stomach gears turn, suddenly self-conscious of all your rust.

"Dang nozzle!" You hear the voice but all you can see is a man's boots sticking out from under the bench. "Ahha!" He crawls out and sits on the floor, fiddling with a cylinder-shaped device.

His hair reminds you of the Watchman's after you shocked him, except Maze's is wispier and white like a cloud. He lifts thick goggles to the top of his head, revealing clean circles around his eyes. Every other part of his face is plastered in soot.

The cylinder pops with a familiar sound.

Your stomach gears turn harder. The man's holding a butane torch like the one the Maker uses to solder metal. It pops again and ignites with a soft roar.

The man looks up, grinning. "Are you fireproof?" he asks. He rolls to his feet and starts toward you while turning the torch up to a loud burn. Before he can reach you, you scurry up to the shelf with the golden cat. She hisses, setting her cloth aside. Despite her glare, you huddle near her, figuring she's still alive after living with Crazy Maze.

"Not fireproof then." Crazy Maze shuts off the torch. "How about dartproof?"

He's fast. Way faster than the Maker. A dart whooshes through the air and thuds into the wood behind you.

The cat hisses again. "You almost hit me, dear Maze."

"My deepest apologies, Amalia," Maze says, yet he launches another dart and this time you dodge.

The cat dodges too, and you collide with her. There's the familiar buzz and before you can jerk away, *zap*! The feline's metal zings and she howls. The purple glow of her eyes takes on a dangerous gleam.

You scamper farther up the shelves before she regains her feet. Behind you comes a growl and the shelves shudder with movement.

"Amalia, wait!" Crazy Maze yells.

The growl continues but the movement stops. You peek over the edge of the shelf. The cat hangs just below, her thin claws sunk deep into the wood.

She gracefully lowers herself to sit one shelf down and continues to glare. Right then and there you decide that if she launches at you again, you'll take a flying leap and hope your wings work.

"The dragon could power the cannon!" Maze says.

Your head swivels toward the man, certain you misheard, but judging by the look on his face, he's serious.

The cannon?

"Dear Maze," Amalia says, "there's something wrong with the dragon. You want it triggering the cannon by accident?"

"Ah, but maybe I can fix it. Let me take a look?" The question's aimed at you and Maze is gesturing at his bench like he wants you to fly to it.

You remember Captain Blake's encouragement to be bold. Rising to your full

height, you spread your wings. Rust falls in a shower of flakes but the metal plates snick against each other like knives on a whetstone. There's a faint huff and you hear Amalia mutter, "How unfair," just before you take a leap.

You glide smoothly, not having to flap even once, and land with a small stumble on the bench. Your claws dig into the wood for purchase, but you don't think Maze will mind. The bench is more scarred than the Maker's.

"Now what seems to be the problem?" Maze asks.

Maze finishes tightening the last screw on your chest plate and taps a finger against your metal. Nothing happens. There's no buzz or vibrations.

"That does it!" he exclaims, sharing a grin with you. "The Captain always brings me the best projects. It's never taken me five days to fix something before. Now," he picks you up and sets you on a shelf between his books on physics, "rest here for the night and tomorrow we'll test the cannon."

He tosses his screwdriver into the bag under the bench and collects his jacket before heading up the stairs to his own room. Moments later, his steady snore echoes against the stones.

Although Maze told you to rest, your

paws tremble with excitement. Maze said he'll keep you if you can successfully power the cannon.

A soft thump warns you a moment before Amalia appears on your shelf. She sits, her long tail covering her paws, and her purple eyes glow in the moonlight coming through the window over the bench. For once, she seems uncertain.

"Have you ever heard of the Emerald Lakes before?" she finally asks.

You shake your head.

"That's where I was supposedly made. I'd like to see them but they're hard to reach. You have to be able to fly to get there, you see." She lays down and tucks her paws against her chest.

Has she befriended me because I can fly? you suddenly wonder.

As though she's reading your thoughts, she says, "You probably think I'm being nice because I want something from you. That's partially true. I also just struggle to make friends. People are…peopley, you know."

You tilt your head in curiosity. At least she's being honest.

"You can stay here and attempt to power Maze's cannon. It'll probably work. But be warned, I've also seen it overpower gem-hearts before." She shrugs but you can't help a shudder. "Or we can fly out that window and find the Emerald Lakes. Beyond that, I'll explore with you if you like. I know lots about the world from all these." She tilts her chin at the shelves upon shelves of books.

As the silence lengthens, you realize she'll wait all night for your answer if that's what it takes.

If you stay with Maze, go to page 101
If you leave with Amalia, go to page 107

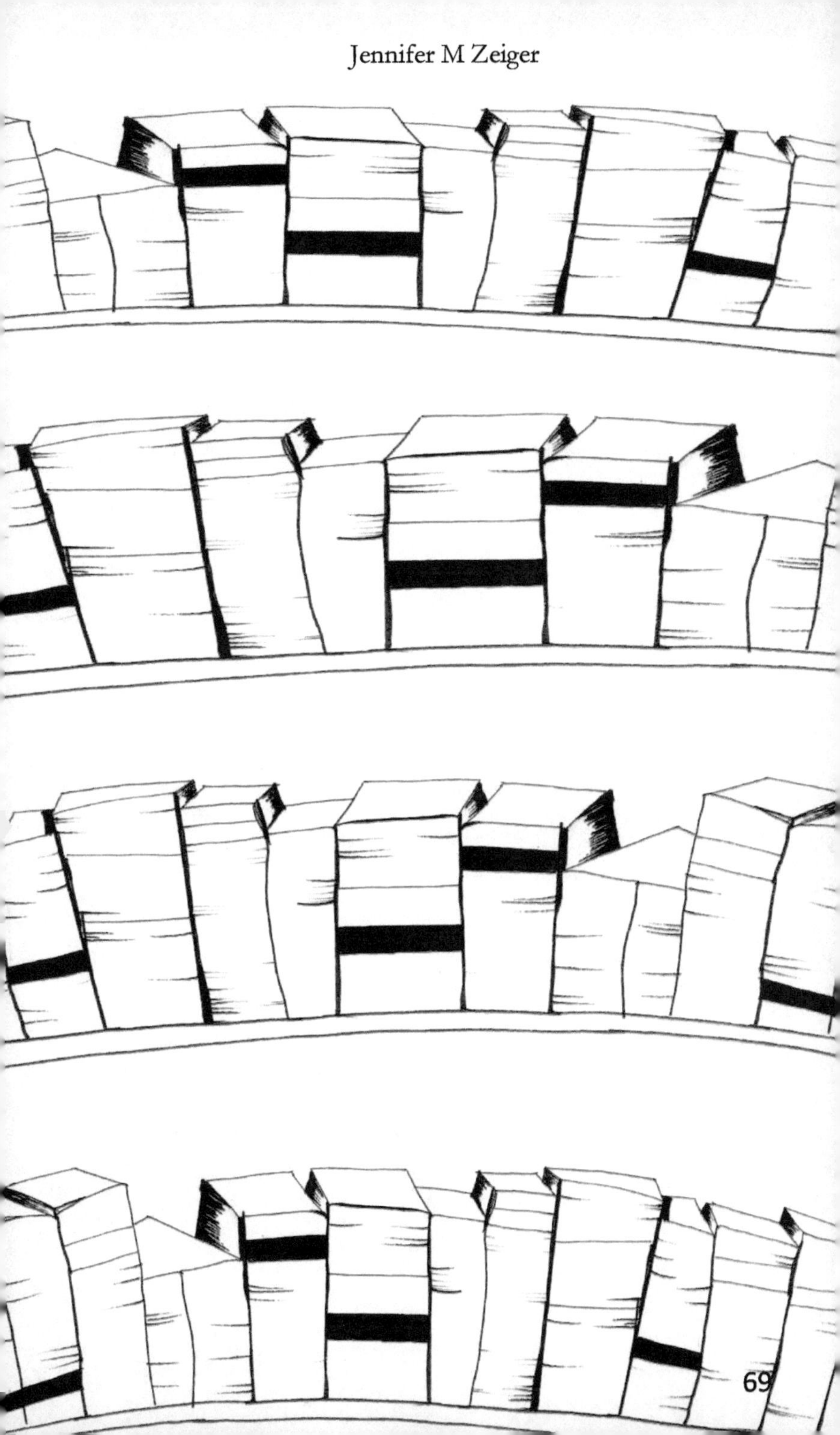

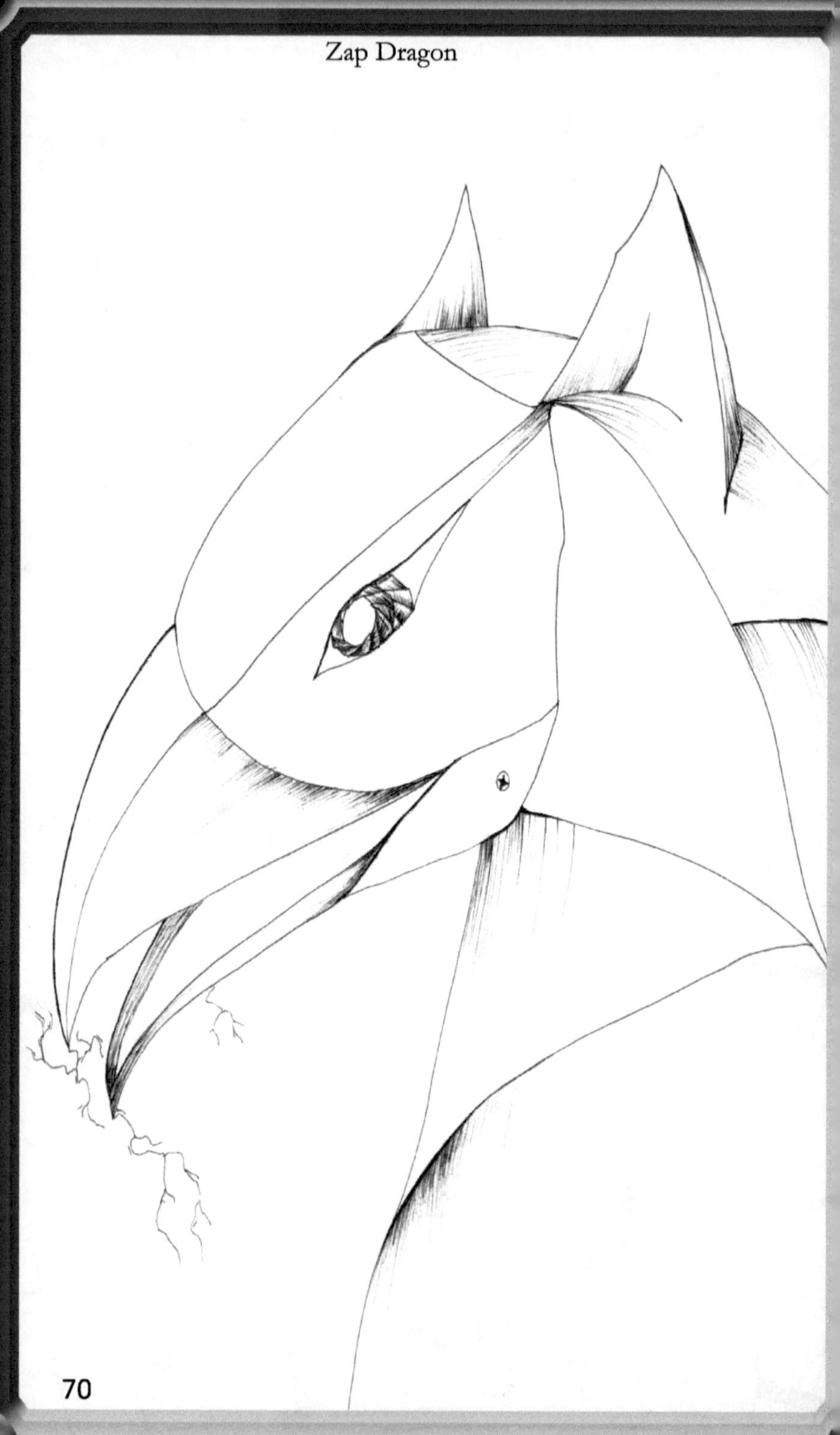

Crazy Maze's tower looms like a giant ready to squish you. Everything about it from its dull gray stones to the gaping doorway fills you with dread. Titan bites the chunk of rusted metal that's sticking out of his paw and pulls it free with his beak. He spits it into the tall grass. You glance behind him at the woods.

He must read your intent a moment before you dart for the trees because the griffin pounces, pinning you under his massive paws. A triumphant grin displays the sharp edge of his beak. The grin's replaced a second later by a curious tilt of his eagle head as your chest begins to vibrate.

If ever you wanted your defect to go full bore, now would be the time. Titan's weight is sinking you into the soft dirt under your wings. As if the defect hears your wish, a resounding *ZAP* rattles your screws and makes your teeth clamp together with a screech.

Electricity bounces from the top of Titan's beak into the bottom. He flies backward, hitting the base of the tower so hard it shakes.

You roll to your feet and take off running. Behind you comes the thud of Titan's pursuit. He's got a much longer stride and you know you won't make it to the trees before he pounces again. You can practically feel him breathing on your back when you spin suddenly and slam your tail against his chest.

His massive wings flare in surprise. Your first guess about him being made of aluminum proves true as your heavier steel dents in his chest plates and sticks. The familiar buzz rattles your screws again and zings out your tail. It's not as strong as the first time but it's better placed. Titan twitches and slumps into a heap in the grass.

You don't wait to see if he rises again. Instead, you take off into the trees where you find the red mouse waiting. He places a toe over his lips, soundlessly asking for silence, and leads you away.

"It's a dragon."

"Who put Titan on the ground!"

"But it's a dragon."

"And that's worse than a phoenix?"

You stand in a glade not far from Maze's tower surrounded by automaton creatures, including a brass sphinx, a steel gray hedgehog, a crimson phoenix with feather plates so thin you want to move closer just to see if they're real, and two mice including your red friend. They call themselves the Rusted Bandits. They all ran from Crazy Maze's tower despite having dangerous defects of their own.

The phoenix bursts into flames. Those thin feathers are hollow in the pinions and fire spurts through them when he's angry, or scared, or…highly emotional for any reason.

The red mouse, Francis, stomps over to stand beside you. "I vote the dragon stays!" He almost puts a paw on your shoulder, hesitates, and places it on his hip instead. "Who agrees?"

"I do!" The hedgehog jumps up with a paw in the air. When he lands, his body shudders and everyone takes a quick step away before hundreds of spikes sprout out of his back. He ducks in embarrassment. "Sorry, guys." The spikes recede as fast as they appeared.

"What has four legs, wings, and a tail, that zaps griffins in the chest?" the sphinx asks.

"It's an easy yes or no, not a riddle," scolds Grayson, the other mouse and the one who's not too sure about you joining the group. At some point he lost the metal plate covering his right shoulder joint and he stands sideways, away from you, guarding the gap.

The sphinx shrugs. "Can a creature of unusual make find a home in the Merchant Forest among strangers?"

"That's a yes!" Francis says.

Grayson snorts.

"You can have the tip of my tail to cover your shoulder," you offer. It wouldn't be hard to remove the end piece that caps your tail. It's a curl of steel that could be flattened for Grayson's shoulder. As for you, it'd be a simple matter of crimping the next link to create a new end.

Francis bites a paw in excitement, looking back and forth between you and Grayson.

"Deal," Grayson finally says. "Come this way; I'll get you a screwdriver."

You share a smile with Francis and follow, thinking a screwdriver could be very helpful. Besides giving him the piece of your tail, you've got some screws loose from your encounter with Titan.

"So, what do the Rusted Bandits actually do?" you ask Francis.

"Oh, it's great!" he jumps up and down. "We find rusted metal in the forest and use it to ambush Titan."

The End

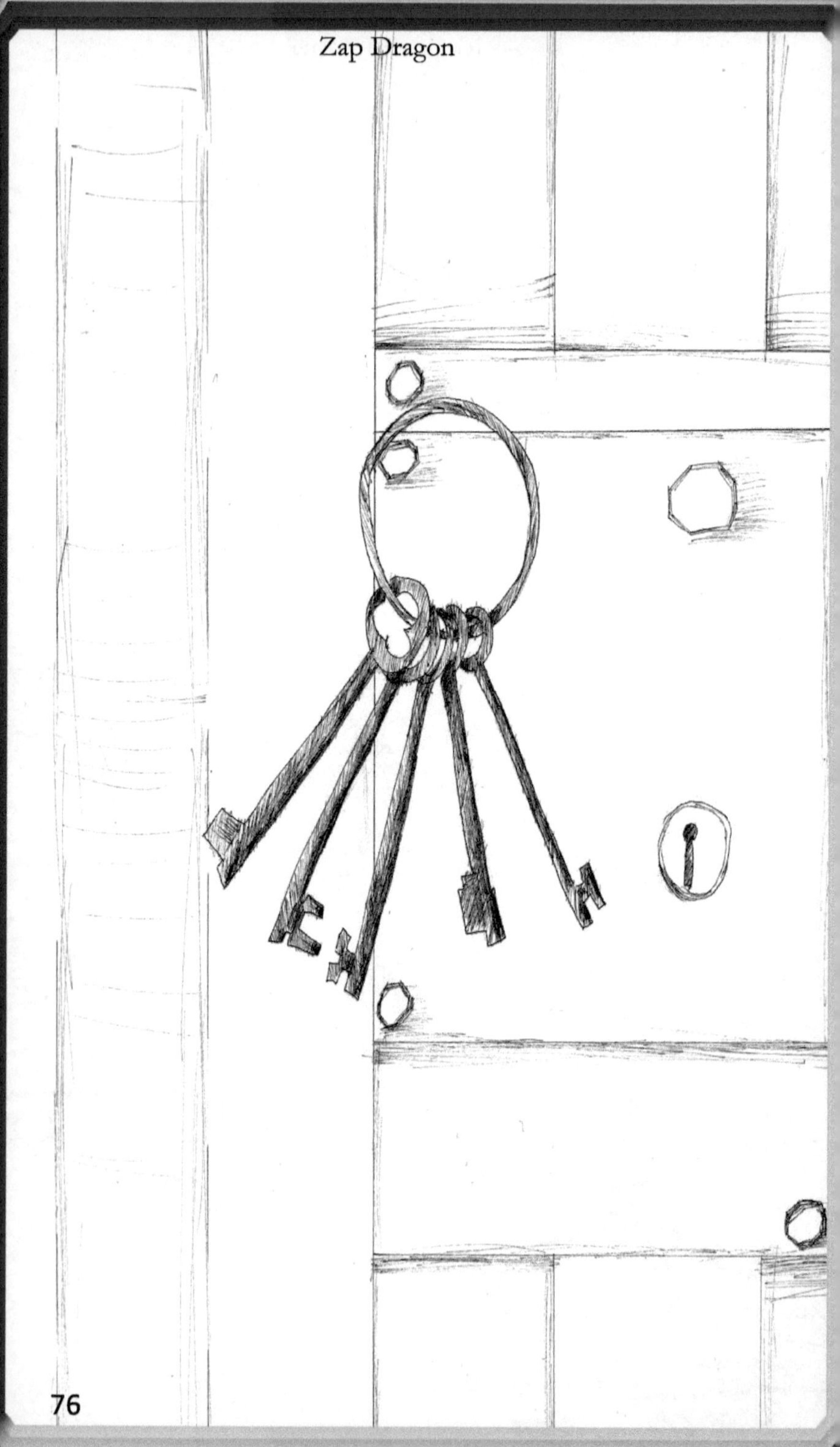

You've never been asked for help before, and it warms your metal that the Captain's willing to trust you. You just don't agree with his plan. All your life you've zapped people at the wrong moments. You'd rather not rely on your defect now when the stakes are so high.

Curling your tail upward, you angle it toward the lock on the top of your cage. The bandit holding Captain Blake glances over and you freeze, realizing how guilty you look with your tail in the air.

Then you have a thought. Some of the dragons in the Maker's shop would curl their tails around items—cabinet nobs, display racks, even other dragons—when they were excited. You grin, clutch the bars in front of you, and curl your tail around the bars above like the happenings in the jail are the most exciting events you've seen in days.

He snickers and returns his attention to the man with the keys.

The Captain, on the other hand, watches as you slowly, ever so slowly, insert the end of your tail into the lock and begin turning it. You can almost see the gears turning in the Captain's head as he realizes what you're doing. He looks away to keep from drawing attention to you.

There's resistance in the lock and then a faint click. The Captain scuffs his boot on the floor, hiding the noise while you test the lid of your cage to make sure it'll swing free.

It lifts without resistance.

Now or never, you think and shove the lid open. With a hop, you're up on the edge of the cage and lunging at the man with the keys. The stack of cages smashes to the floor behind you but you're focused on your target. He looks up, surprised.

In that moment, you know your jump wasn't strong enough. You're going to hit him mid-torso instead of closer to his head as you'd hoped. You instinctively spread your wings. They slide open with a sharp, metallic snap. You've never flown before, but it feels natural to flap against the air resistance flowing under the metal plates.

The resistance grows stronger and suddenly you rise on a powerful upthrust, right into the man's chin. He stumbles and you latch on to his jacket. There's the jingle of keys followed by a faint thud as they hit the floor. You barely hear it over the shouts and commotion, but you release the bandit with a hard shove and drop to the floor.

Luck's with you. You land beside the keys, scoop them up, and take off running, dodging boots and chair legs until you reach the desk and duck beneath.

It's then that you see the Captain's

predicament. He's spun around and he and the prisoner are choking each other through the bars. But the prisoner is a bigger man with a longer reach and Captain Blake's face is turning red above the bandit's big fist.

The other Watchmen can't help as they're occupied with subduing the rest of the bandits.

You have to help the Captain but you can't take the keys with you. You tuck them up into the bottom of the desk and then scamper back across the jail floor, dodging feet again as you go.

You duck through the cell's bars, zeroing in on the gaping hole in the bandit's boot. Extending a sharp claw, you stab the bandit's toe and jump away.

He howls.

Your chest buzzes and zaps harmlessly.

The Captain seizes the distraction and knocks the bandit's head against the bars. When he steps away, the huge bandit slumps into an unconscious heap on the floor.

Captain Blake's pen makes scratching noises as he fills out his report about the capture of Boss Gingham and his gang. From where you lay on the corner of his desk, the writing looks like scribbles, but from the look on his face, it's important stuff.

Finally, he leans back with a sigh.

"Got a question for you," he says.

You raise your head from your paws, surprised he's talking to you.

"I can't fix your problem, but you did nicely in helping us today. I might be able to convince the Watch to take you on as a Watchdragon. Or there's an eccentric artisan, Crazy Maze, who lives out in the Merchant Forest. He might be able to fix you, but I'd have to give you to him. Which would you prefer, Watchdragon or Crazy Maze?"

If you pick Crazy Maze, go to page 59
If you pick Watchdragon, go to page 83

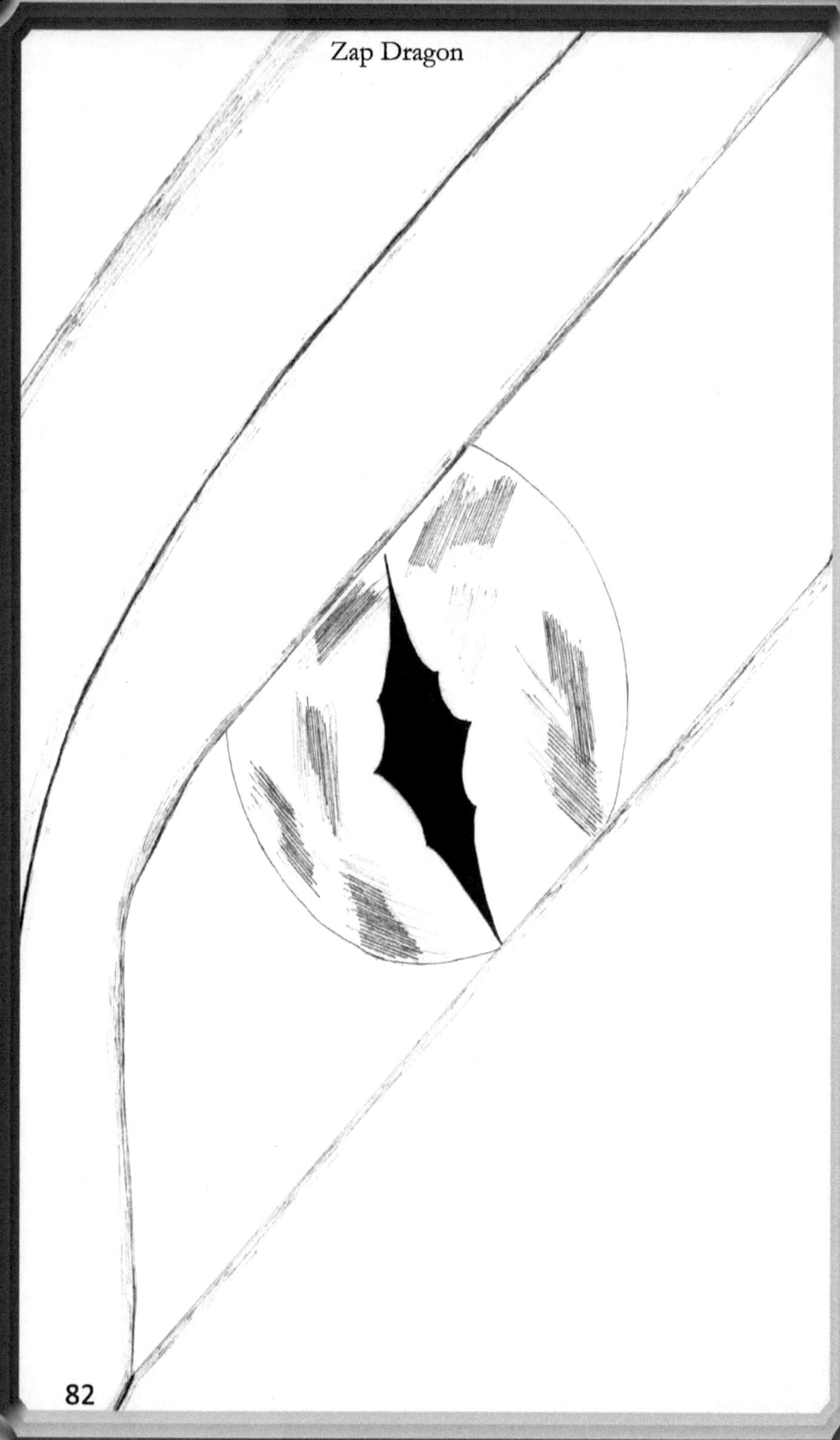

You never realized how big the city was, but now as you patrol with your new partner, Carson, you gape at the ambling streets and the passing carriages in unashamed awe. Surprisingly, despite zapping him in the alley, Carson volunteered to be your partner. He's the only Watchman besides the Captain to do so.

"They don't know what kind of protection you'll offer," Carson nudges you where you ride on his arm. He wears heavy leather gloves and thick padding to protect him. So far, it's been enough to keep you from sending him flying onto his backside.

You try smiling and he grins back. "Does all that smudging on your eyes cause you problems?" he asks.

You tilt your head curiously and your metal creaks. Carson gave you a rag and some oil to work on your rust, but you haven't had the time yet to finish the job. "Can't remember a time it wasn't there," you admit.

A passing gentleman frowns and hurries away. Carson doesn't seem to notice but it's not the first instance where your talking seems to startle people.

"Let's find out." He withdraws a handkerchief from his pocket and carefully scrubs at one eye. For once, the contact doesn't trigger the buzz in your chest. When he draws away, your eyes grow wide. "I'll take that as a yes," Carson says and cleans the other eye.

With both marble eyes cleaned, the day seems brighter despite the growing gray of dusk elongating the shadows in the streets.

"This is the industrial quarter," Carson explains as he continues walking. You leave the busy shopping district and enter a nearly deserted section of large brick buildings. "We've gotten complaints that the dockmaster's warehouses are being raided of gem-hearts. Just like the one that powers you," Carson taps your chest. You're surprised he's so willing to risk your defect. Carson keeps talking like his interaction with you isn't unusual, "So the Captain's set up a few spots for us to keep watch the next couple of nights…"

You half listen as you continue to gaze around in wonder. Large red brick buildings now line the street and farther down the avenue rise the masts of ships. You've never seen ships before and are about to mention that when movement at the corner of the warehouse ahead catches your eye. You haven't encountered another person in over five minutes.

"We're being watched," you whisper.

Carson doesn't miss a beat. "Can't have thieves taking stuff from our citizens, you know…" he keeps talking and crosses the street, heading into an alleyway between the warehouses.

As soon as you're out of sight, he ducks behind a dumpster and crouches, waiting for anyone to follow. While you wait, he sets you down and you peek under the metal bin. You can't help but notice the similarities to when the Watch caught you. Alleyway, dumpster, unfriendly people.

But now you're not alone.

You spot the two men when they enter the alley, loosely clutching pistols.

"Can you zap the dumpster when I ask?" Carson whispers.

"I'll try," you say. You explained to him earlier that it doesn't always work on command, but he nods and peeks around the dumpster. Then he finds a loose stone and pitches it into the metal bin.

It clangs like a bell.

"Caught us a Watchman," one of the men chuckles. "He won't be catching any thieves tonight."

Your paw shakes as they draw closer.

Please work, please work.

"Don't gloat until we've got him," the other man scolds.

You lay your paw on the side of the metal bin. You can't see anything but their feet now but they're almost on top of you. They reach the dumpster and pause. A moment later, you hear them flip the lid open.

"Now," Carson whispers.

Please work!

You focus inward to that spot that always vibrates right before electricity shoots out of you. Nothing happens. No buzz, no vibration, not even a tingle. Frustrated, you flop onto the ground and drop your paw.

The familiar vibration rattles your chest. You slap the dumpster a second before the electrical *zap* sings from your metal. It's not strong enough. You know it even as the men hop back with startled cries.

Carson rushes forward with his baton but freezes when one of the men raises his pistol. The thief gestures at the open dumpster. "Get in."

Carson slumps and climbs into the bin.

You can't help him with the gun trained on him, so you cower into the shadows. If the men don't notice you, you might be able to help Carson after they're gone.

Your hope disappears, however, when one of the men moves around the dumpster and motions with his pistol. "You too."

Drooping, you climb up the side by sinking your claws into the metal. Each step makes a high-pitched screeching, but you're not worried about making sound now. Finally, you flop over onto the old newspapers in the bottom of the bin.

Not wasting time, the thieves drop the lid and metal grates against metal while they secure it somehow. One slaps the side and the bin vibrates, setting your teeth on edge. "Sleep tight, Watchman." Their footsteps recede down the alleyway along with their muffled voices.

"Sorry," you say when the silence grows too long.

"Sorry? What have you got to be sorry for? This is your first day on the Watch." Carson sounds…excited?

"But we failed and now we're stuck."

Carson laughs. "We've seen the thieves' faces," he says. "Come tomorrow, their likenesses will be posted all over the city. As for being stuck, I saw what those claws of yours can do to this metal. It shouldn't take long for you to free us."

You flex your long claws. Carson doesn't view this as a failure. He doesn't even think of it as a setback.

Sinking your claws into the side of the dumpster to climb toward the lid, a grin grows across your jaws. "Exciting first night," you say, suddenly enjoying your first experience as a Watchdragon. Then you ask, "Can we go see the ships sometime?"

The End

After months of hiding in the discard heap and then getting thrown into the dumpster, you can't just lie on the carriage seat and let Lady Mae decide your fate without at least attempting to influence her decision. It's time to be bold.

You open your mouth, and a whine comes out instead of words.

"Oh dear." Lady Mae sits up straighter, startled.

You cough, gears grinding, and try again. "Ke—keep me…please." You tack on the "please" as an afterthought, remembering customers saying it when they were making their selection at the Maker's shop. It always seemed so polite, and Lady Mae strikes you as a polite kind of person.

She blinks. The longer she's silent, the more you wish you could cower somewhere. With your wings stuck open, though, you're not even sure you can roll to your feet without help. Maybe if you slide off the carriage seat, you could land upright on the floor? What then? Can you get out of the carriage?

You're about to try it anyway, certain you crossed a line, when Lady Mae says, "I'm not sure Sir Leo's daughter will be able to fix you. Are you okay with that?"

You nod, scared to speak again.

Lady Mae thumps the roof of the carriage

and yells to Geoffrey, "Head to Sir Leo Mason's, please."

Soon after, you stand in Sir Leo Mason's foyer beside Lady Mae. You rock back and forth, listening to a rattle coming from your belly. Something is loose inside of you. Lady Mae and Sir Leo both eye you and you stop, embarrassed.

They go back to their polite conversation as they wait for the butler to fetch the gentleman's daughter.

Sir Leo strokes a hand down his bright red beard. With so much facial hair, he's hard to read, but you think he's slightly amused, judging by the crinkling skin around his eyes.

Footsteps echo on the floor and a young girl appears, skipping down the steps.

Disbelief freezes your gears. It's the girl from the alley. The one who saved all the other dragons from the street boys with her shock baton. A tiny dragon on her shoulder seems to be eating the nub of a wax candle. It stops eating to eye you but goes back to chewing after only a moment.

"Eira, Lady Mae has a request of you," Sir Leo tells his daughter.

Lady Mae crouches down and points at you. "This one had an unfortunate encounter with a transformer. Think you can fix the wings? I'll compensate you for parts."

Eira runs her slender fingers over your left wing, inspecting it. "Plates are fused. It could be expensive to replace them. Is that all right?"

Lady Mae nods. "I'll be back in a few days."

Once Lady Mae and Sir Leo leave, Eira considers you closer. "You're a bit big for me to carry. Can you walk?"

In answer, you waddle toward the stairs, your belly rattling with each step.

Eira's tiny dragon watches from the corner of her bench while she works. Her small shop has the familiar smells of glue, copper, iron, and sawdust. She works with a quiet efficiency that already has one wing fixed and the other one almost done and it's a day earlier than Lady Mae requested. A thrill runs through you. All fixed up, Lady Mae will surely keep you.

"I'll move onto that rattle next," Eira mutters as she files a burr off your new wing.

You glance at the tiny, wax-eating dragon. He pauses from chewing his current candle nub long enough to belch a small jet of flame and then goes back to eating. You haven't seen the other dragons Eira saved but from comments between her and her papa, you know she's been working to fix them as well. Considering her work on your wings and the defects she's fixing on the others, she's good. Really good.

Can she fix your defect?

Eira steps back and extends your wing for inspection.

You decide to be bold again. "I zap people," you say. "I don't mean to, but I shock people when they touch me. Can you fix it?"

She glances at where her fingers are holding out your wing.

"Hasn't happened since I ran into the transformer," you explain.

She chews on the end of the file and then nods. "I'll look into it."

"Right beside the dragon's gem-heart, there's a power-gem," Eira explains to Lady Mae a day later. "I think the artisan was playing with a defense mechanism but the power-gem's too strong for the wiring he installed and it shorted out." She holds up a mass of singed wiring that she pulled from inside of you the previous night. "The dragon's encounter with the transformer disconnected the harness altogether. I put in new wiring and reinforced the protective cage around the gem-heart. So far, that seems to have fixed the problem. If you have issues with it, let me know."

Lady Mae smiles and it lights up her

narrow face. "Well done." She hands Eira a bag of coins.

"Such a dragon would make an amazing bodyguard," Eira suggests. You wonder if she's thinking of how handy her shock baton was against the street boys.

"A bodyguard?" Lady Mae pauses, considering. "That's a fabulous idea."

As you follow Lady Mae from the manor, you glance back. From the front door, Eira watches with her tiny dragon on her shoulder. She winks and you wink back. A bodyguard! Now that's a job where your shocking nature will come in handy!

The End

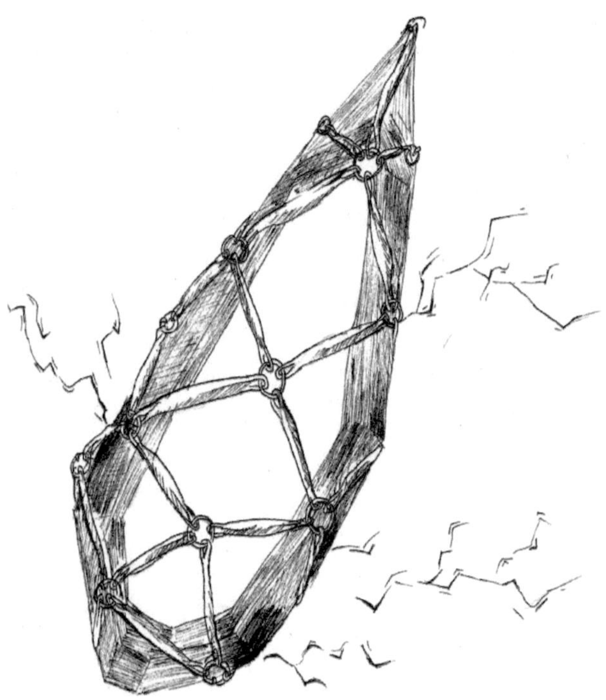

You'd dearly love for the Maker to finish your design. Lady Mae seems kind, but you keep your jaws shut and think of all the Perfect dragons in the Maker's shop. It's possible you could join them and find a home too.

Lady Mae taps her lips again and then sits up straight to thump the ceiling of the carriage.

"Take me back to the dragon artisan's shop," she tells Geoffrey.

The carriage turns. Not long after that, it stops and Lady Mae carries you into the familiar shop. Your gears ache with nerves but you hold still.

"How may I help you?" the Maker's familiar voice asks as he steps up to the counter where Lady Mae set you down. With your wings stuck open, she laid you on your back and you refrain from trying to stand despite how awkward it is to look up at the Maker's chin.

The Maker likes a quiet and orderly shop. He does not like dragons moving or speaking.

"This poor creature met a transformer this morning. Would you be interested in it?" Lady Mae asks.

"May I?" he holds out a hand, asking if he can pick you up and inspect you.

"Of course," Lady Mae says.

The Maker takes you to the bench along the back wall. You're not sure what he's doing until he again lays you on your back and starts unscrewing the screws that hold your chest plate. It's then that you realize he recognizes you despite giving up on your design months ago.

He opens the chest plate and a soft ruby glow lights his lined face. You know from seeing him work on other dragons that it's your gem-heart, the ruby that powers your design. Added in with the ruby light is something else, a greenish tinge, but it's faint and you're not sure what it is.

There's a look of surprise and interest in the Maker's eyes as he turns back to the counter. "I'd love to take this one off your hands," he says.

He and Lady Mae agree on a price and she leaves.

Your nerves grow stronger as you look around at the shelves of finished dragons above the bench. A couple of them stare back at you, their eyes glittering, but they know better than to move in the Maker's shop.

Then the Maker's back and he pulls a pair of pliers off the wall. With them, he pulls a small green gem from inside of you. A mess of wires hangs off the gem, but you can still see the black singe marks beneath.

"Least the cage around the heart's

good," the Maker mutters. He removes the metal wiring and scrubs the gem clean until the green glow you noticed earlier lights up his face.

"Maybe copper would work better—" he wanders away and returns with a spool of wire.

As the hours tick by and the Maker's expression gets more and more aggravated, you realize he's not going to be able to fix you. With shaking hands, he tries again to place the emerald into the new copper harness he made. He pauses, setting his tools down to rub his hands, and then starts again.

There's a crack and the Maker grunts. His hands shake even harder as he pitches the now dull green gem into his discarded gem box. He starts screwing your chest plate back in place, pauses, grunts again, and instead dumps you into his newly growing discard heap on the floor with only two screws instead of six.

He shuffles around cleaning up, flips off the lights, and leaves.

Silence settles over the shop. You're surrounded by bits of leather and small chunks of metal that the Maker must have thrown in the heap before you arrived. It's not a large heap, but there's enough for you to settle into while you think.

Now that you've seen outside the shop, you're fairly certain you could do just fine out there. Your defect's gone too. As far as you can tell, that green gem, a power-gem from your guess, was the source of your problems.

You eye the quiet shop and all the Perfect dragons sleeping on their shelves. The first task, if you're going to make it outside on your own, is to find new wings. The Maker removed your old, fused ones while tinkering today.

You and the other Discards got thrown into the dumpster that morning for the very thing you're considering: sneaking around at night searching for parts. Although you didn't participate while they'd searched, you watched.

With growing determination, you decide you can do it. You can find new wings, replace your missing screws, and escape. If the Maker doesn't want to finish you, that's okay, you'll finish yourself.

You give the shop another scan. Certain all the Perfect dragons are sleeping, you slip from the small discard pile. Approaching the wall that's covered with wings, you consider which set would work best for your design.

The End

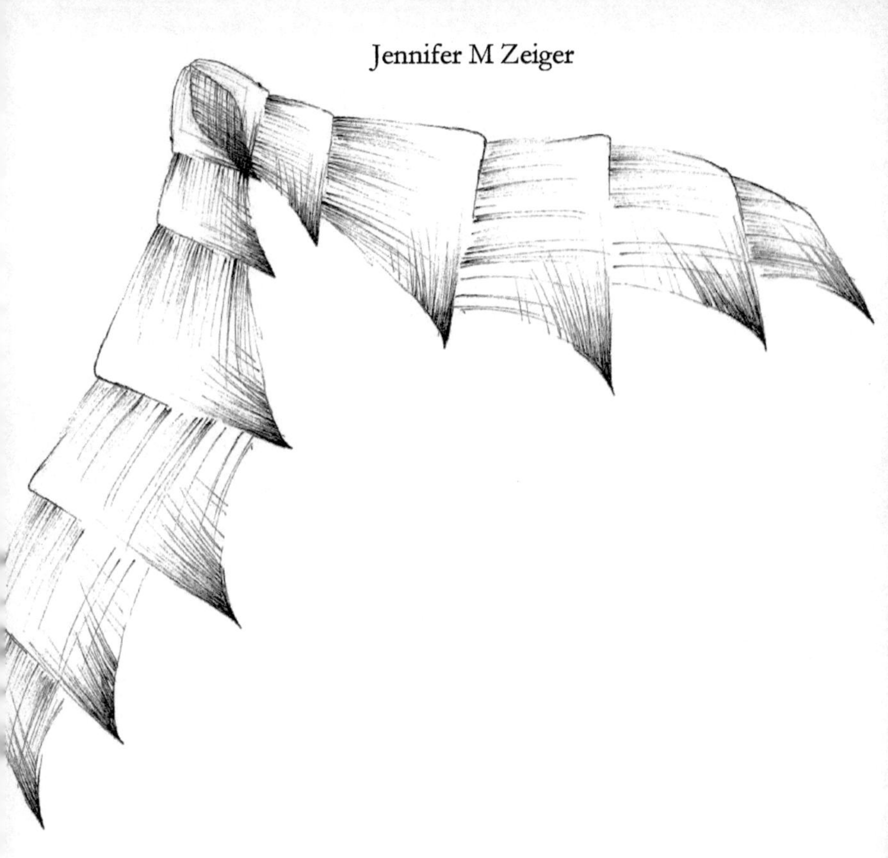

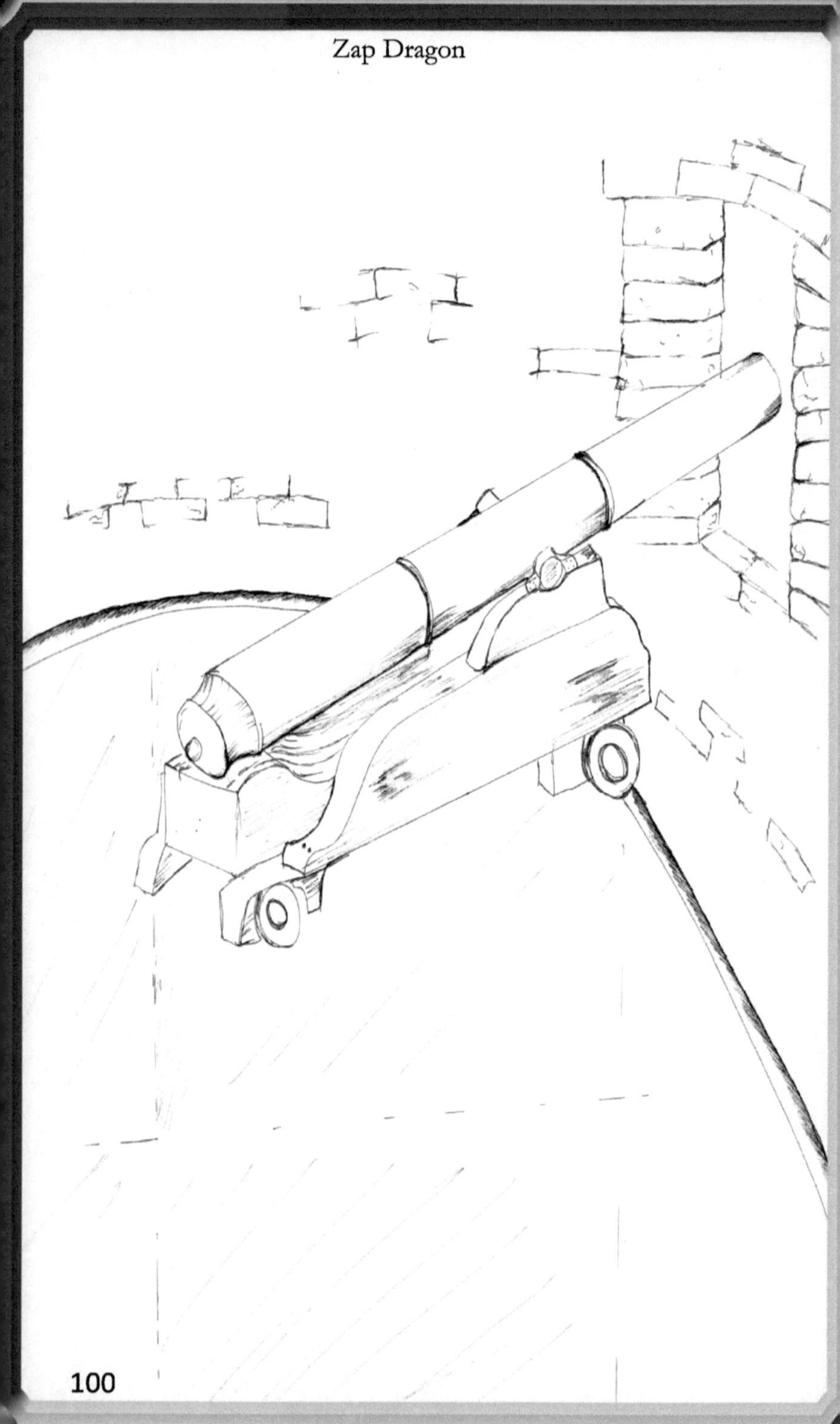

$\mathbf{A}$ part of you would love to explore the world but as you look at the stacks of haphazard books and tools, at the well-used bench and the winding staircases, you realize you already have far more than you ever hoped. Maze's tower could be a home for you instead of just a place to exist. And, to top it all off, you're curious to see if you can indeed power Maze's cannon.

Amalia must see your decision without you having to speak it aloud because she sighs, stands up, and returns to her spot two shelves above. Although the disappointment in her purple eyes almost makes you reconsider, you finally lay your chin back on your paws and allow sleep to overcome you instead.

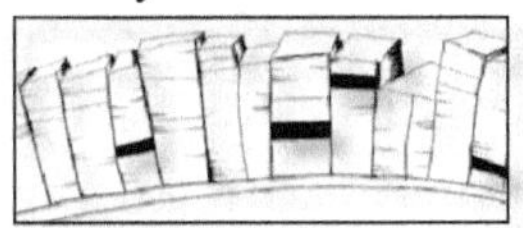

"Wakey, wakey," Maze says, prodding you with a finger the next morning.

The tower's filled with sunlight. Maze drinks coffee from a clay mug and the light highlights the steam off the top. He gestures for you to follow. He's been having you work on your flying, so you spread your wings with a sharp snap and follow in flight as he heads up

the small flight of stairs that circles the tower to a room above.

You've never been in the room before.

It's a much smaller circle than Maze's shop with only one item inside: a large cannon that sits on a track that can be swiveled around to face each of the six windows in the tower walls.

"This," Maze presents with a flourish, "is the cannon."

"What's it do?" you ask. As far as you know, the city doesn't have any nearby enemies.

Maze eyes you. "Can you keep a secret?" he asks.

Who would you tell? Amalia? She's standing at the top of the stairs, apparently wanting to see if you can power the cannon too, but not wanting to be any closer.

You nod your head. "Of course."

"We're one of four towers," Maze says. "With the advance of technology such as yourself, other nations have gotten it into their heads to send automatons into the city to spy on us. This," he pats the cannon, "shoots them down before they enter the city."

"How do you know they're enemies?" you ask.

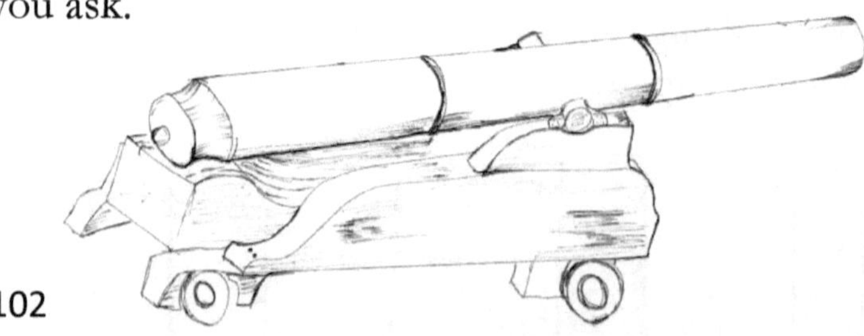

"Ah, you're smarter than people think you are! The gem-hearts powering each of you are found here and only here. The other nations use their own means for creating automatons. They're a poor substitute but they work…sort of. The cannon won't harm a true gem-heart, but it'll drop a lesser automaton."

"Plus," Amalia speaks up, "their automatons don't think. They follow a programmed routine and fly home. All machine, no heart."

"Okay," you hop, flap, and land on top of the cannon. "What do I do?"

Maze cranks the barrel around to the closest window, the one that faces farther out into the Merchant Forest.

"Stand here," he says, indicating a spot farther back, "and place your paws here." You wrap your paws around the bar he indicates. "When you're ready, trigger your defense mechanism and—"

Although Maze fixed your defect, it still doesn't take much to set it off. At the mere thought of it, your body tingles and—

Zap!

A whoosh of what looks like watery air jumps from the far end of the cannon. It bows the tops of the trees you can barely see out the window. Beneath you, the cannon bucks and you fly backward to smack into the stones of the tower.

The world sparks and as everything goes black, you think, *this is it.*

"Wakey, wakey," Maze pokes you. Instead of a mug of coffee, he's eating a chicken and cheese sandwich. A piece of tomato drops out the bottom.

"I'm not dead?" you ask.

"Nope," Maze answers, retrieving the tomato. "Just not quite right on the insides. I reworked your wiring and now I think you'll be able to power the cannon like a champ. You ready to try again?"

The End

You've never considered exploring the world beyond the city before but even your short experience in the Merchant Forest showed just how much more there is to see. Now that Maze fixed your defect, you're not worried about interacting with others. But then, leaving seems like a poor way to thank Maze for his work.

"What about Maze?" you ask Amalia. "He fixed me."

Amalia sighs and reaches under the shelf to pull out a small leather bag. When she shakes it, the contents jingle. "I've worked for Maze catching mice for five years," she says. "I've never had a reason to spend the money I earn."

"What about my flying?" you ask next. You've been practicing by circling the ceiling in the tower, but you're still quite wobbly. "I'm not sure I can carry you."

Again, the cat reaches under the shelf and pulls something out. She unravels it to reveal what looks like a bag with leather straps. "It's a harness," she explains, "so you can carry me beneath you, and I won't interfere with your wings. Want to give it a try?" At this question, her amethyst eyes sparkle in excitement.

"When did you have time to make that?"

She just grins. As you're coming to realize, Amalia likes to be prepared.

"Let's try it."

You don the harness with her help and she crawls inside. She's not much bigger than a large rat. When she attacked you the first day, her ferocious nature made her seem much bigger.

"Here goes nothing," you say but hesitate.

"What's life without a little risk?" Amalia asks.

Gathering your courage, you leap. Amalia sways in the harness, pulling you precariously to the left. You almost clip the shelf with a wing before tilting back toward the well-worn workbench on the far side of the room.

Amalia peeks out, her ears perked up to sharp points. "Try climbing."

You do and, after a few powerful beats, you reach the room's ceiling and soar in a circle. Amalia laughs and you feel the harness quiver with her excitement.

"Now try to land."

The suggestion sounds simple but as you approach the bench, you realize you're going to have to land on your hind paws first and carefully come down on your front to keep from squishing Amalia. And the swing of the bag isn't going to help.

At the last moment, you flap your wings to bring yourself to a brief pause, and then set down onto the wood of the bench. It's smooth until you step on the harness and flop awkwardly onto your stomach.

Amalia giggles. "Try again?"

You do and by the third time, you manage to land without squishing the cat.

Amalia whoops softly. "You're a natural, dear Zap." She started calling you that the first day after you shocked her. "Ready for some exploring?"

You both look at the window. Climbing up onto the sill, you gulp. The outside of the tower seems to go on and on before reaching the ground. It's a much farther fall than the bookshelves.

"Tell me again about the Emerald Lakes," you say.

"The lakes are so clear they turn blue in the sun. They go on for miles…"

You leap off the windowsill while Amalia talks. Chill wind buffets your wings and for the first time in your life, you're flying the open world.

If you could see the future, you'd know that you and Amalia make it far beyond the Emerald Lakes, spawning myths about the Zap Dragon and the Golden Cat. But you can't see the future. All you can see is the night sky and the Merchant Forest spanning before you. And you know it's a beautiful night to start an adventure.

The End

Zap Dragon

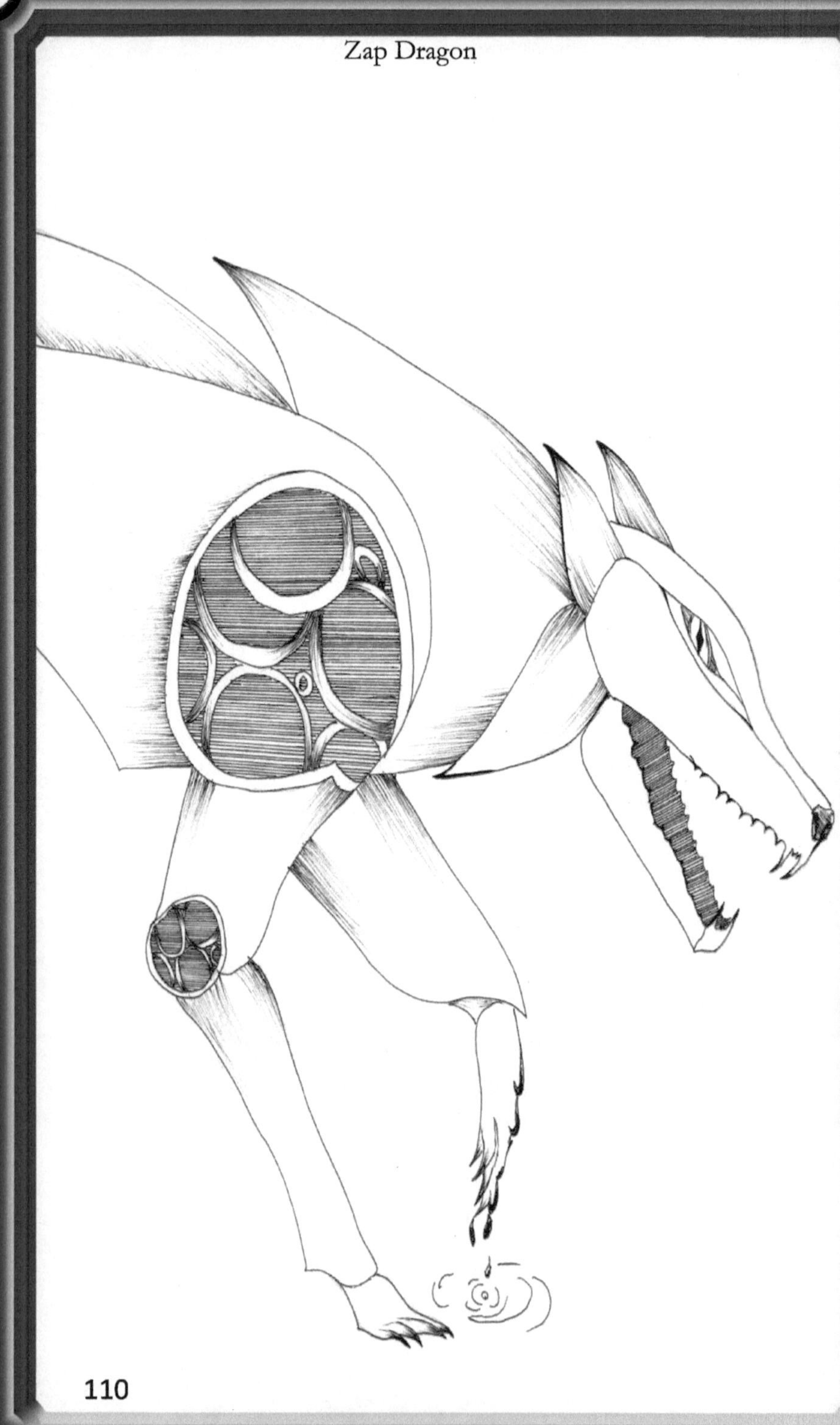

The narrowing tunnel is tempting but you're not sure you're fast enough to reach a spot where the wolf can no longer follow. You scamper left toward the gate with the unconscious rat in your paws. His extra weight throws you off balance and you careen off the wall before recovering. The blow scrapes your elbow but at least it doesn't set off the buzzing in your chest.

There's a soft thump in the tunnel behind and a growl. You stretch your legs out farther, urging more speed.

As you run, your paws begin to sink into the mud and the musty smell you first noticed grows particularly strong. The mud starts to suck up between your toes with a squelching *slu-ick, slu-ick, slu-ick*. It threatens to glue you to the floor. With each step, it pulls at the connections on your claws.

There's a louder, faster *slu-ick, slu-ick, slu-icking* coming from behind and a whimper escapes you just as you reach the gate. Now that you're closer, you see the bottom half is buried in silt. You drop the rat onto a mound of moss on the far side of the gate and spin to grab the bars.

The gate budges a few inches and stops with the silt piled up along the bottom. A few tugs prove it's not moving farther unless you can clear the base.

Down the tunnel, orange eyes glitter in the dark. "Caught a couple of snacks," the wolf taunts.

You don't respond as you cast around for something to clear the mud. There's nothing besides your paws, so you start scooping as fast as your arms can handle. Each swipe digs muck between your metal scales but finally your claws find the bottom of the gate. Giving one last heaping scoop to be sure the silt's low enough, you grab the gate and heave.

Its rusted hinges scream but it swings and thuds into place just as you can make out the wolf's outline in the dark. His ears lay back at the screeching metal. He lunges but before he can swipe a paw through the bars, you shove the locking bar into the floor and snap the lock shut.

You're barely in time as you back away. The wolf presses his nose against the far side of the bars. His jaws open in a toothy grin and you hear the hum of his gears through his open mouth. "Only a delay, little morsel, only a delay."

Your paws shake. You move to check on the rat but find the mud glued your feet to the floor in the few seconds you paused after locking the gate. With a monumental heave, your feet *sluick* free enough for you to grab the moss mound where the rat still lies unconscious. Hauling yourself up beside him, you lean close.

Did you kill him? You place an ear near

his side and breathe in relief when you hear the faint whir of his gears.

The wolf rattles the gate and you freeze, afraid the rusted metal will give under his weight. For now, it holds. But you don't trust it to last. Hopping on moss mounds, you wander farther down the tunnel to see where it leads. An itch settles between your wings, right in the middle of your back, and you're sure the wolf's watching.

He starts to chuckle.

The tunnel continues for another ten feet, and then comes to a caved-in dead end.

"Backed yourself into a corner," the wolf taunts, still chuckling.

You lean on the jumble of crushed bricks, thinking maybe you can dig out a hole, but nothing gives. They're so tightly wedged together that the water trickling toward them is pooling at the base instead of finding an avenue through.

You return to the rat and sit down, trying to ignore the glow of the wolf's eyes. Maybe he'll give up and go away. You don't know what else to do.

Hours later the wolf still hasn't given up. Occasionally, he shoves a shoulder against the gate and it rattles, raining down rust into the water below, but thankfully the old metal still holds—for now.

The rat, Claud, sits beside you. He woke not long after you locked the gate, gears twitching and red eyes flickering until his body finally settled back into a normal rhythm. He only introduced himself after you convinced him electrocuting him was an accident.

The wolf smacks the gate with a paw again and it rings like a bell.

Claud squeaks and jumps to his feet. He's halfway up the wall before he realizes the wolf didn't break through.

The wolf laughs.

Claud slumps back to the moss mound and shudders.

You give him a commiserating look.

"Hold tight," you whisper.

"How?" he squeaks. "We're trapped."

The whole time the wolf's been staring at you, you've been thinking about that. You just got out of the Maker's shop. The world's open to you if you can get past the wolf.

Beyond the bars, the wolf's amber eyes begin to dim and hope sparks within you. If he dozes off from boredom, you might have a plan.

You and Claud are small enough that,

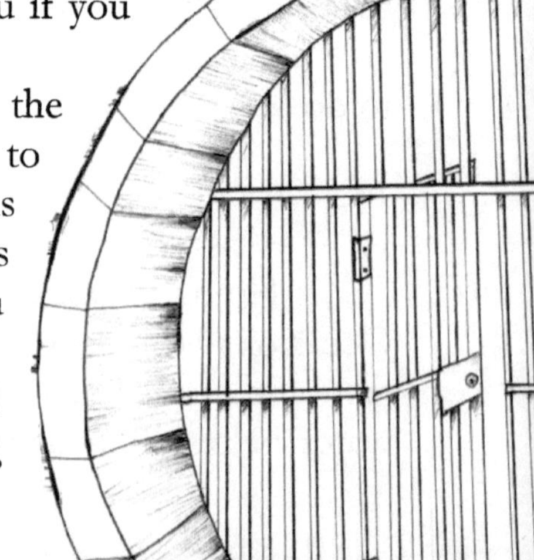

unlike the wolf, you can slip through the bars of the gate and sneak past. It's a huge risk. No matter how quiet you are, you're not sure you'll be able to sneak past without waking him.

Considering, you shift positions and the thick mud *slu-icks* around your toes. When you raise your paw, brown globs drip off your claws like glue starting to set.

You eye the water trickling past the bottom of the gate. A different idea occurs to you. If you back up the water under the pretext of making a dry spot, it'll pool around the wolf's haunches. He's so big that he might not think about the extra muck gathering around him. If you can get it thick enough, it might glue him to the floor, which, if he does wake while you're slipping past, will give you a little extra time. You hesitate, however, as any movement until he's fully asleep might draw his attention.

If you only sneak past, go to page 123
If you mire the wolf first, go to page 129

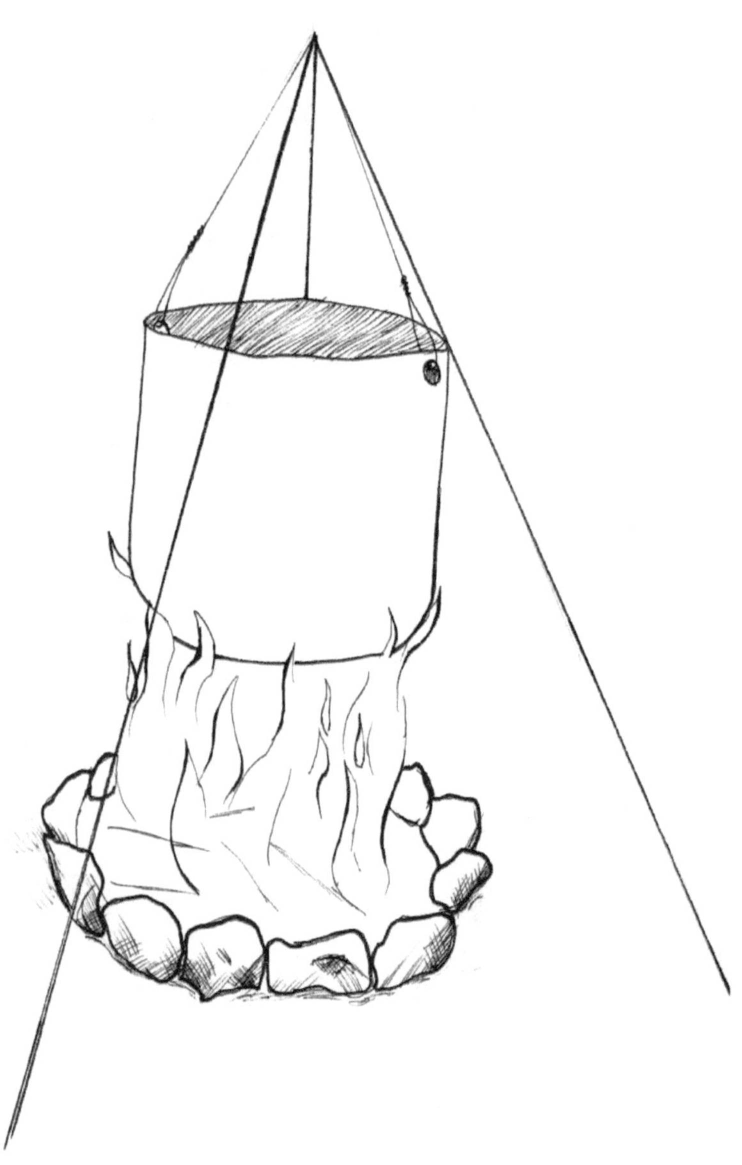

Even from where you stand, the metal gate looks rusted. It's questionable how long it'd hold against the wolf's considerable bulk. You take off down the narrowing tunnel, coaxing as much speed from your legs as possible.

You stumble and catch yourself on the wall with an elbow. Although you're unwilling to leave the rat behind, he's awkward to run with in your paws.

There's a thump and a growl behind you.

The tunnel suddenly dumps into a massive five-way intersection. You couldn't see it previously because, from a distance, all you could make out was the tunnel directly across the way. You skid to a stop on the slimy floor and the musty smell shoves its way down your nose. The tunnel directly across does indeed narrow like you hoped, but so do two of the others.

"Pssst!"

The sound hisses along with the drip of water.

"Psst!"

Finally, you spot a small nose with fiber whiskers sticking out of the tunnel to your left.

"This way," the rat beckons.

You turn on a heel and follow the creature just as a howl vibrates the walls. The tunnel the new rat takes you down immediately narrows into a small channel. Your shoulders scrape against the walls and you have to tuck your wings tight to your sides. You begin to wonder if you're going to get stuck when the rat says, "It's not much farther."

Despite the tight tunnel, you don't need the encouragement. You can hear the wolf's claws still scraping behind you.

"Here." The rat turns, leading you to a red wooden door hanging off the ceiling's bricks like a business' shingle. He pushes under it and holds it open for you. The room beyond takes your breath away. After the tiny tunnel, you can suddenly stand to your full height. To your right, a small fire adds warmth and light. Beside it, a golden rat stirs a kettle of something sweet smelling.

Along the left wall are small nests of cotton and leather, each with a tiny wash basin and a mirror. There's a gray rat curled on one of those nests, reading from a book twice his size.

"Mazel, grab the electrodes! Claud's out cold!" yells the rat who led you into the room. Now that you can see him better, you make out his bluish steel gears and polished claws. Unlike the rat you're holding, there's not a spot of rust or oxidization on him.

"On it, Argus!" the golden rat near the fire, Mazel, cries as she scampers to a cabinet on the back wall.

The reading rat thumps his book

closed and wanders over.

"Name's Horace," he introduces himself. "Glad you found Claud." He gestures at your paws. "We started to wonder when he didn't return from fixing a pipe in section C. Look at those green spots! He must have gotten lost."

"What happened?" Argus asks as he gestures for you to set Claud on the floor.

It's hard to tell them that Claud's "out cold" because you zapped him, but you don't want them finding out about your defect the hard way, so you explain about the wolf and everything else.

"The wolf, eh?" Argus rubs his chin as you finish.

Mazel arrives with a wooden box. Peeking out of the top is the shimmer of a green gem covered in some sort of harness. Wires that end in metal clips extend from it. Mazel attaches the clips to Claud's front paws and stands back.

There's a hum and Claud's red eyes snap open. "Whoa!" he shouts. "That's a jolt."

"Leave him attached for a bit," Argus instructs and returns his attention to you. "Come join us by the fire." He leads the way to the fire and Mazel returns to stirring her kettle. This close, you see it's full of some oily substance.

"Helps our gears," Mazel whispers, noticing your attention on the pot. "Here, this'll help you with your rust." She hands you a piece of sandpaper. "It'll take off the rough spots and then you can oil the steel."

That would explain why Argus is so shiny. You've seen the Maker polish his dragons just like she says.

"We've been having more and more issues with that wolf lately," Argus says.

"Almost got me last week when I was clearing a drain," Horace grumbles.

A shudder travels your long spine at the thought of dealing with the wolf all the time. You curl your tail around and start sanding the rust that covers the tip. As you work, you keep your wings well tucked to keep from touching anyone.

"Maybe," Argus continues, "we can do something about him if you're willing to help."

Four pairs of rats' eyes turn to you with a glimmer of hope.

"What are you thinking?" you ask, moving up to the second link in your tail. Mazel nods her approval.

"We've been planning an ambush," Argus admits. "There's a spot that we've rigged to electrocute him if we can lure him into the water. Not sure if it'll actually take him out though."

"Or?" you ask because you can see Argus is still thinking.

"Or there's an open cage on the docks

that we might be able to lure him into. The Watch has been trying to capture him for months now, but none of them are willing to enter the sewers, so they haven't succeeded. None of us," he gestures at the rats, "can get up to the cage for the last leg of the path. We might be able to lure him by getting him to chase us to the chute—it's a storm drain—but someone who can fly, or who can jump like the wolf, will have to do the last part. Then we can turn him over to the Watch. What do you think?"

You're all for helping them. As you consider which way sounds more promising, Mazel spoons out a cup of the oily substance and hands it over for you to sip. "Helps the internal gears," she says.

The cup warms your paws while you consider.

If you go for the electrocution trap, go to page 137

If you go for the Watch's cage, go to page 143

Zap Dragon

The wolf's eyes dim further but don't totally go dark. If you start moving around now, the chances of renewing his interest in tormenting you are pretty high.

"Wait until he's asleep," you whisper to Claud.

The rat nods and huddles down into the moss like maybe he can hide there.

Trying to pass the time, you pull a paw from the muck and let the sludge drip from your claws. Claud does the same and you both begin making shapes with the drips as they leave little dimples in the mud. The activity's small and doesn't seem to draw any undue attention from the wolf. He huffs and rests his chin on his paws, just staring with boredom dulling his gaze. You dunk your paw again and pull up more muck.

Time drags but when you glance up a while later, the large beast's amber eyes are almost dark and his breathing steady. Automatons don't have to sleep, but most follow a regular schedule like humans. And most will doze off when bored.

You continue dripping mud but watch as the amber glow dims even more. It's just like back in the Maker's shop when the Discards waited for the Perfects to fall asleep on their shelves before sneaking out to find parts. Except this time, the consequences of waking the

sleeper will be higher.

But you don't plan on waking the wolf.

The amber eyes finally dim to dull orange orbs and the wolf's breathing steadies into a deep rumble.

You nudge Claud and he squeaks softly.

"Shhh." You place a claw over your lips and roll to your feet.

Cautiously, you approach the gate and peer at the beast. His breathing remains steady. It ripples the water under his nose.

Claud squeezes between the bars first and presses his back to the tunnel wall to slip past the wolf.

You do likewise, holding your wings as tight to your body as possible and releasing all of your breath. This flattens your torso and allows you just enough space to slide between the bars without scraping your chest plate again.

Muck sticks to your paws as you shuffle sideways along the wall. You don't want it to *slu-ick* like it did when you were running, so you try to keep your motions low, walking through the silt rather than lifting your paws high enough to step over it. As you move, you eye the elysium plates that make up the wolf's body. They fit so seamlessly that it takes a moment to spot the tiny screws holding them in place.

You're about halfway past the wolf when there's a hitch in his

breathing. You and Claud freeze, listening for the wolf's snore to resume.

It doesn't happen. Instead, the beast's head shoots up from his paws and he looks intently into the empty tunnel ahead. Then he whips around, catching sight of you.

"Run!" Claud shouts as he bolts.

You try to follow and land on your face. The mud glued your feet to the floor and now your front paws are stuck too. Panicked, you snap your wings open and a wingtip connects with the wolf's side.

Zap!

It's not a strong reaction, but it's enough to make the wolf flinch.

You flap hard to free your paws from the muck. Instantly, you're scampering down the tunnel.

Claud's nowhere in sight, but unless you want to try flying, there's only one option at the intersection ahead. You scurry on, hoping you're fast enough as the thump of metal paws chases you. You pass the spot where you fell and hit Claud and career into the narrowing tunnel, coming to an intersection you couldn't see before. You haven't reached a narrow enough section to escape the wolf, so you take a tunnel at random.

Moments later, you turn again and slide around a curved bend in the sewer. You drop into a lower section but, when you pause, you can still hear the wolf behind.

Hurrying on, you're not sure when you stop hearing the thump of the wolf's paws. By the time it dawns on you that you're only hearing your own claws on stone, you have no idea where you are in the sewers.

Exhausted, you slump onto a particularly large mound of moss and start tearing at it to still your nerves. It's oddly soothing.

Once you've calmed enough, you look around, trying to figure out which way to go.

Days, weeks, or months could have passed by the time you reach a spot where you can see daylight streaming into the sewer from a grate ahead. You've no idea as you've lost track of time.

Approaching the grate, you pick up the conversation of two men ahead. In your wanderings, you've run into such men before. They work in the sewers sometimes. As a rule, you avoid them, but their words catch you now, making you pause.

"I tell you, there's a new creature down there. It leaves marks all through the moss like it's marking its territory." You look down, realizing you're pulling up clumps of the moss while you listen. "Whatever it is, it's got nasty claws."

"As long as it leaves us alone, I'll take it over the wolf," another voice says. "Maybe it'll even scare it away."

Not likely, you think, but then, as you ponder their words, you find you like the idea of having a territory to call your own. You've never had a space that was yours before. Plus, you haven't seen the wolf since your first encounter with him. Perhaps he doesn't like the deeper sewers where you got lost. Maybe if you stay to the lower tunnels, he'll leave you in peace.

Moving away from the men, you don't notice the growing rust on your metal as you begin to consider the possibility of staying lost— of becoming the new "creature" in the sewers.

The End

Although the wolf's eyes dim further as he continues to stare, he doesn't drop off into sleep. It's not going to matter how much you move around if he's watching anyway.

"I have an idea," you whisper to Claud.

You rise and stretch, making your metal scales creak. Too long in the sewers and you'll rust right through. Muck drips from you, having firmed up the longer you stayed in one spot.

The wolf raises his head.

You begin shaking the mud from your claws. It flies off, splattering the wall.

"What are you doing?" Claud hisses, glancing down the tunnel.

"It's messing with my gears," you say loudly. "Help me create a dry spot."

Without waiting for him, you start pushing the muck toward the gate. When the water and silt start trying to wash back over you, you claw up chunks of moss to create a barricade. There's so much silt and water in between your scales that you can feel it sloshing inside but you're committed to your plan now and don't stop.

Claud scratches an ear, his red eyes glittering. Finally, he gets up to help. As he leans close, he whispers, "What are you *really* doing?"

Smart rat.

You glance over at the wolf. Growing

bored, he's now laid down again with his chin resting on his paws. He doesn't seem concerned about your activity. Nor does he seem to notice the water and mud starting to grow around his body.

"We're gluing him in place," you say, still shoving silt and water through the gate. Between the moss and the metal, a deep, muddy lake is starting to pool in the tunnel on the far side.

Claud bares his sharp teeth in what you assume is a smile and shovels silt faster. In his excitement, he chases the water and silt toward the gate and is caught in the rush of fluid. He slips and slides as he draws close to the bars but can't stop. With a squeak, he slides right through.

The wolf's eyes had begun to dim but suddenly they light up brilliantly orange again. Claud scrambles back through the bars to safety as the wolf lunges. His shoulder slams into the metal and a brick falls out of the ceiling.

A wide grin pulls at the wolf's jaws. Muck drips from his torso but because he didn't stay in place long enough, it didn't have time to set. Pulling back, the wolf slams his shoulder against the gate again. The rusted metal groans and more chunks shake out of the ceiling.

Claud squeaks and races to hide behind you but he doesn't get far. He jerks to a stop with a grunt. "I'm stuck!" he shouts.

Fear freezes your gears as the wolf slams the gate again and a bar snaps.

Claud throws a clump of moss at you. "I'm stuck! Help me!"

You tear your eyes away from the wolf.

Claud points frantically at the mud covering his feet. "Something's got my toes!"

You dig into the mud, trying to feel what snagged him. All you find is more muck and cold brick.

"Hurry!"

The metal gate groans.

Digging your paws in again, you're about to give up and place yourself between the wolf and the rat when you feel something new. Reaching deeper, you grab what feels like a ring. It moves. You're not sure if it's what snagged Claud's foot, but you heave on it anyway and there's a sucking sound as a metal disk comes up in your paw.

Claud stumbles backward.

You flop onto your haunches and drop the metal disk.

The water and muck give a sucking sound and suddenly there's a small whirlpool swirling at your feet. Within moments, the water's gone and small trickles of silt slither down a drain in the floor. Maybe you can escape down it. Apparently, Claud has the same thought because he jumps in without looking.

There's a loud crashing mixed with the screech of snapping metal.

When you look, the wolf leers over the broken gate. Tossing caution away, you're about to follow Claud when you realize you can still see his ears sticking out of the floor.

"There's another grate!" he screeches. You hear his claws scraping against metal.

Something grabs your tail and you're hauled backwards. Even as the buzz starts in your chest, the wolf smacks you against the wall and your defect fizzles.

You land on the floor, sparks dancing across your vision.

The wolf looms, dripping water and muck from his paws like some swamp monster.

To your left, Claud peeks out of the drain.

Your vision sparks again, but when it clears, you realize the wolf stands on the far side of your moss barricade where the water couldn't drain. You snake your tail through the moss to touch the tip into the water.

"Going to enjoy two tidbits today," the wolf gloats.

You focus on that spot inside where the buzz always starts. You will it to work. Instead of a buzz, however, you feel a dull ache.

The wolf laughs.

Claud squeaks and cowers until all you can see is his nose and the tips of his claws.

You will the ache to grow, to be something more, and it spreads along your metal plates, creeping instead of flashing outward. You fear it's not going to be enough. It's going to fizzle and *pop*.

ZAP!

You're jolted off the floor. Electricity snaps out your claws and off your nose and, finally, out your tail.

Your world turns white.

The wolf becomes an outline of light like lightning struck it and lit its body on fire. As fast as it happens, the light's gone and the sewer tunnel's pitch black. There's a resounding splash. A moment later, a wave of muck washes over your body.

"What just happened?" Claud's voice quivers in the sudden quiet.

Finally, your eyes begin to adjust. There's a dark lump in the pool to your right. You search for glowing amber eyes but after several moments of stillness, nothing appears.

"I think I short circuited it," you say.

Claud whoops. He scampers over to check and hesitates with his paw inches from the massive head. Then, with a jerk, he smacks the forehead. The elysium rings like a bell.

The wolf doesn't move.

Claud whoops again and jumps, dancing a jig before scampering over to you. It looks like he's about to hug you, so you flinch away, your plates creaking and your innards sloshing with the sudden movement. You try to stand and your legs wobble, so you flop back down to sit before you fall over.

Claud goes utterly still. "Right! You zappy things. Man, have I got to tell the family about this! You're coming over for supper, right? I have to introduce you to them. They're going to love you!"

Warmth builds in your chest.

"Give me a moment," you say, waiting for your legs to stabilize. Then, once you can walk again, you follow him past the motionless wolf and ask, "What exactly do you mean by supper?"

The End

The rats certainly prepared for this ambush. You wait on the far side of a four-way intersection in an alcove the family hollowed out for just this purpose. Beside you is a lever attached to a power-gem. The lever completes the circuit from the power-gem to thick cables extending into the pool of muck gathering in the middle of the intersection.

The silence is starting to make your scales itch, but you hold still, thinking of poor Mazel and Claud running from the wolf. Your part in the plan is simple compared to theirs.

Argus promised they could lead the wolf to you. All they asked was for you to throw the lever and make sure the wolf doesn't exit the pool by jumping into the chute above the intersection.

For the first ten minutes, you practiced flying up to the chute to make sure you could indeed protect the exit. Not surprisingly, you find flying thrilling and you'd love to keep practicing, but neither do you want to be in the wrong spot when the rats arrive.

So, you huddle in the alcove and wait. The urge to itch at the rust on your paw is distracting. Maybe you'll work on your paws next with the sandpaper when this is over.

A faint scratching catches your ear, and you straighten to your full height to listen. The scratching grows louder and excitement makes your paws shake.

Across the way, you spot Claud's red gem-eyes. To your left, Horace's gray nose and whiskers quiver at the edge of his tunnel, and to the right there's an emerald glow, telling you where Argus stands.

That leaves Mazel.

The rats tag teamed the chase, knowing none of them could keep ahead of the wolf on their own. But by leading him down familiar tunnels, they were able to duck aside when he got too close and the next rat would jump out farther along, enticing him to keep up the chase.

Mazel shoots into the intersection and scrambles your way, her chest heaving. Behind her, the wolf splashes down, missing her by inches. Mud splatters up his black metal legs and across his belly.

As soon as Mazel clears the water, you throw the lever. It pops and one of the cables smokes.

"It shorted!" Mazel squeaks. "Keep him in the water." She scurries to the smoking cable and starts fiddling with it.

The wolf's head swivels toward her voice and his amber gem-eyes lock onto you. Panic gives you an added boost as you snap your wings open and jump into flight. You flap hard for the chute at the top of the intersection.

The wolf laughs. "I like this game." He jumps.

On instinct, you bank sideways, and his claws rake your belly. It sends you whirling uncontrollably into the wall, which oddly helps since it stops your spin. Snapping your wings out, you regain stability and peer down at your chest.

Deep grooves mar the steel and one of your screws seems to be missing. There's no time to consider the damage further as the wolf is now stalking toward Claud, who exited his tunnel to draw his attention.

There's a *pop* and everyone freezes.

Mazel squeaks. Her paws, nose, and chest are now covered in sooty streaks from the electricity that just shocked her. She huddles back over the cable, trying to get it attached back to the power-gem in a way that won't short again, but now the wolf's eyes are locked on her instead of Claud.

"Watch out!" you cry.

Mazel looks and bolts but doesn't move fast enough. The wolf pins her to the ground under his massive paws. Her metal creaks under the weight. If someone doesn't do something fast, the wolf will be after Mazel's gem-heart.

You fly at them and, at the last moment, tuck your head and slam into the wolf's side. It's like hitting a solid wall but he steps sideways, just slightly, to steady himself. It's enough. Mazel squirms free and races away.

Your defect *pops* harmlessly as you slump onto the floor. Your vision sparks. The wolf spins and pins you in Mazel's place. He's so big that his body blocks any access to the power-gem and the cables leading into the pool.

The pressure on your chest makes your metal scales ache. There's a ping as a plate breaks loose and another screw goes flying. Even if all the rats charge him at once, they don't have enough weight to shove him off. You know in that moment that the only hope is your defect.

You will it to work and there's a familiar buzz in your chest. Instead of instantly zapping out your scales, it builds, rattling your screws.

The wolf tilts his head and leans closer like he's trying to listen. You latch onto his snout with both your paws just as the buzz within you fires.

ZAP!

Usually, the electricity hits and is gone like lightning. This time, it shoots out your chest, through the wolf—you see it spark around his eyes—and back into your paws where you hold his snout.

Your gears freeze in place and the buzz builds to a hum that hurts.

You hear Mazel shout, "Take cover!" a

second before your world disappears.

Mazel peeks out of her tunnel only when the debris stops raining into the intersection's pool.

"Oh no!" she whispers.

The alcove where her battery used to stand is a blown out hollow. There's no sign of the wolf who almost killed her or the dragon who saved her.

Argus solemnly wanders over to the spot and picks something up. He turns it toward Mazel as she approaches. An emerald hue glints at her.

"It's a piece of a power-gem," she says. "Must have been part of the dragon's design."

"Saved our hides, that dragon," Argus says, rubbing his chin after handing the shard to Mazel. She clutches it in her paws. "Today shall be known as the Zapping Dragon's Day, in honor of our friend," he announces as the others join them. "Let's sing a dirge."

As they wander home, their small voices echo through the sewers in a haunting lament for the dragon who saved their lives.

The End

Above you rises a large chute, a storm drain just like the one you dropped through when you shocked Claud. Except this one leads to the surface and faint daylight filters down to create a circle on the moss-covered floor. The rats certainly prepared ahead of time in hopes of capturing the wolf. You wait in a small alcove in the tunnel wall that the family hollowed out for just this purpose.

Above the chute lies a cage the Watch placed in the shipping district where they hoped to capture the wolf. They tried luring him into the cage through its door in the side, but the wolf avoided the opened door every time and the Watch eventually gave up, leaving the cage behind to retrieve later.

When Argus noticed the abandoned cage sat directly over the sewer drain, he had the family cut out a hole in the bottom to align with the chute. Argus figures if you and the rats can lure the wolf in through the bottom, he won't see the trap until the rats have latched the drain's hatch closed behind him.

Your paws shake with nerves. They're encased in leather gloves that Mazel stitched together. The whole plan relies on your ability to fly up that drain. You practiced earlier to make sure you could indeed get to the top but it's a tight climb and you scraped your wingtips a few times on the walls. The feeling of flying, however, is fantastic. You'd love to keep practicing, but the wolf has to believe you stumbled across a rat and are trying to steal it from under him.

As you wait, the silence starts to make your scales itch, but you hold still, thinking of poor Mazel and the others running away from the wolf. Your part in the plan is simple compared to theirs.

Argus promised they could lead the wolf to your location by tag teaming the chase. None of the rats can run fast enough to stay ahead of him, so instead, they planned a route where one rat could duck aside when he got too close and the next rat could jump out farther down the sewer, enticing him along.

You huddle in the alcove and wait, trying to calm your nerves by thinking of your scrap of sandpaper and cleaning the rust off your paws. The open hatch of the drain catches your eye where it rests against the wall. It swings upward to close the drain. A heavy task for the rats but Claud and Horace rigged a pulley system hooked to a pile of bricks so they can knock it over quickly and seal the hatch once you lure the wolf above. From where you wait, you can just barely see the rope peeking out of the moss Argus used to hide it along the wall.

A faint scratching catches your ear, and you strain to see down the tunnel. Mazel should appear at any moment.

Argus picked her because she's the smallest and she'll be easier for you to carry. The scratching quickly grows louder, and you know for certain that it's a rat running your way. Mixed with the scratching comes a growl that echoes against the walls.

Mazel comes into view, her chest heaving for breath. Moments later, the wolf's lithe form appears behind her.

As Mazel draws closer, you flex your paws in the gloves and get ready to spring. Just as she enters the circle of light at the bottom of the shoot, you pounce, grabbing Mazel and winging past the open hatch and up the drain.

A howl echoes after you. "That's my prey!"

You wing harder. A glance back shows the wolf's angry amber eyes glowing below. He gathers himself to jump.

A wingtip scrapes a wall as you turn your attention back upward. You wobble but focus on the light above that's growing closer. One more strong flap and you're out of the drain and into the cage above.

"Faster!" Mazel warns.

There's a thump behind you. Never in your life have you seen an automaton that can jump like the wolf. He doesn't even use the side of the drain to span the distance. He lands almost on your tail and snaps his teeth, barely missing your wing.

You pull harder, clutching Mazel close but keeping her from touching your scales. With one last flap, you tuck your wings and sail through the bars and out of the cage.

The wolf hits them right behind you, shuddering the entire frame. The bolts that hold it to the ground shudder but hold. He tries one more time but when they don't budge, he spins, heading back for the hole in the cage and the drain.

You haven't heard the hatch close yet. Argus, Claud, and Horace need more time. You're close enough to the ground that you drop Mazel the last few feet and holler, "Hey!"

The wolf pauses.

You grab the cage above him and slam your tail against the bars.

Zap!

Electricity sings through the cage and fills the air with the sharp smell of hot metal. The wolf bares his teeth.

You jump away, snapping your wings open to catch yourself as the wolf takes a swipe.

A metallic boom from the drain produces a cloud of dust that erupts from the ground. The wolf snarls, realizing his escape has been closed. He rams the bars with a shoulder. The cage shudders but holds.

Mazel moves up beside you, eyeing him. "When Argus had us cut that hole in the bottom of the cage last week, I scoffed at the idea that rats could lure that beast into it. I guess with the help of a dragon, anything's possible."

That evening you sit beside the fire in the rat's cozy home and sand at a spot of rust on your forepaw. Across the way, Mazel works to open a can of oil and Claud slumbers in his nest against the wall.

Soft conversation drifts into the room and a moment later, Argus and Horace pass under the red wooden door.

"The Watch was mighty excited to find the wolf in their cage," Argus announces. "Horace here wrote them a note to let them know about it."

Horace beams and his whiskers quiver.

"Now," Argus says, settling down beside you at the fire, "how about we see if we can figure out that zapping issue you have?"

The End

Banking hard to avoid a collision with the bakery's wall, you turn right and wobble when one of the street boys jumps for you. His fingers brush your legs.

He growls.

You growl right back, and don't see his friend until the boy smacks you in the side of the head with his shoe. You sail into the wall of a carriage and then land on the road, dazed. Wheels rumble by. Their crunching on the road sounds inordinately loud.

Just as you're blinking your sight back into focus, the taller street boy swoops down with his burlap sack. It closes on you and then the world's swaying oddly as he picks you up. Only small pinpricks of light show through the dark fabric. You shove your claws through the sack, intending to claw your way out, and hear a yelp.

"Got a cage? This thing will claw out in no time!"

Your world spins and sways and then the sack's set down on a hard surface. There's a clear, definitive click. When you slice open the side of the sack, you find yourself in a wooden cage with three sets of eyes staring in.

"Hah! Today's not been worthless after all," says one of the boys. "Look at all those parts! We'll be rich."

Your stomach gears churn as the boys pick up the cage and wander back into the alleyway.

You huddle within your cage and watch the three boys where they sit at the back of the tavern's basement. This must be their hideout because they knew how to sneak in through the window and they have a small nook set with sleeping mats.

The establishment must use the place for their cold cellar because shelves of cheeses and canned goods fill the chilly space. From your spot you can make out peaches and pickles and beets. A general murmur of voices comes from above but you're more focused on the boys' conversation. While eating their pilfered bread and cheese, they're discussing what to do with you.

"Those wings alone will fetch a gold piece on the docks if we polish off the rust."

"Yeah, but we need to detach them without getting electrocuted."

You shudder, glad for once for your defect. It's probably the only reason you're still whole.

"Gloves," the third boy says. He hasn't spoken much and the other two fall silent at his suggestion. "We'll want leather gloves. We'll have to snatch some from the stable."

They finish off their bread and scramble through the window by climbing on a stack of crates. It's only after the window thuds shut that you shift out of your huddled position. The stables can't be far, so this is probably the only opportunity you'll have to escape. You slide your tail out of the wooden cage and insert the end into the padlock.

"Psst!"

You freeze.

"Psst! Down here."

You snake your head between the bars to look below you. There's another cage. Inside sits a long dragon missing his tail and one of his wings.

"Name's Arti," the creature says. "Think you can get my lock too?"

You glance toward the window. There's probably enough time. You twist your tail until your padlock clicks. Moving on to Arti's, you open his in even less time.

"Fantastic!" Arti slides out and immediately flops onto the dirt floor. "Oops," he says. "Forgot about my tail."

"Let's go." You head for a different barred window you noticed behind a stack of potato crates. You

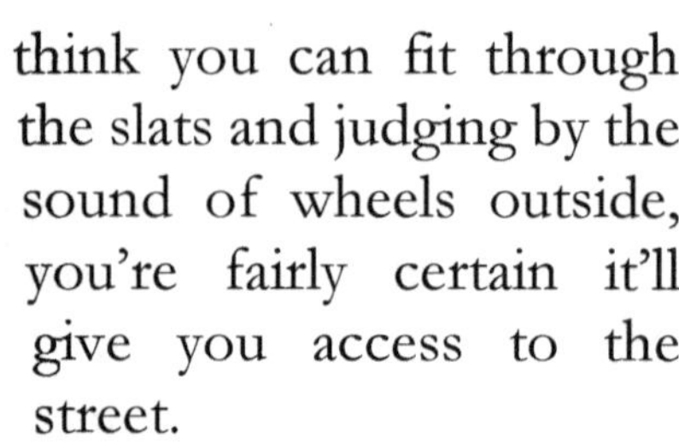

think you can fit through the slats and judging by the sound of wheels outside, you're fairly certain it'll give you access to the street.

You're halfway up the crates when the boys' window thuds again. Since Arti's just below you, you know it's not him. You look over your shoulder anyway and meet the eyes of the tallest street boy.

"Hey!" he shouts, throwing the leather gloves he carries.

They smack into Arti and the dragon squeaks. He loses his hold and thuds onto the floor.

Everything in you wants to clamber up the crates and out the window.

"Help!" Arti cries.

You can't leave him.

If you join Arti on the floor, you might be able to race with him through the room to the door on the far side of the basement. The boys will be hesitant to outright touch you because of your defect. But that means you'll be racing right into their feet too.

A smell catches your attention. It's musty. Sniffing, you're led to peek into the crate you're clinging to. Inside sits a pile of potatoes. You could toss the potatoes at the boys and give Arti time to join you…as long as Arti can move fast enough before the potatoes run out. Then you both can scramble out the window to freedom.

If you drop to the floor, go to page 155
If you throw potatoes, go to page 161

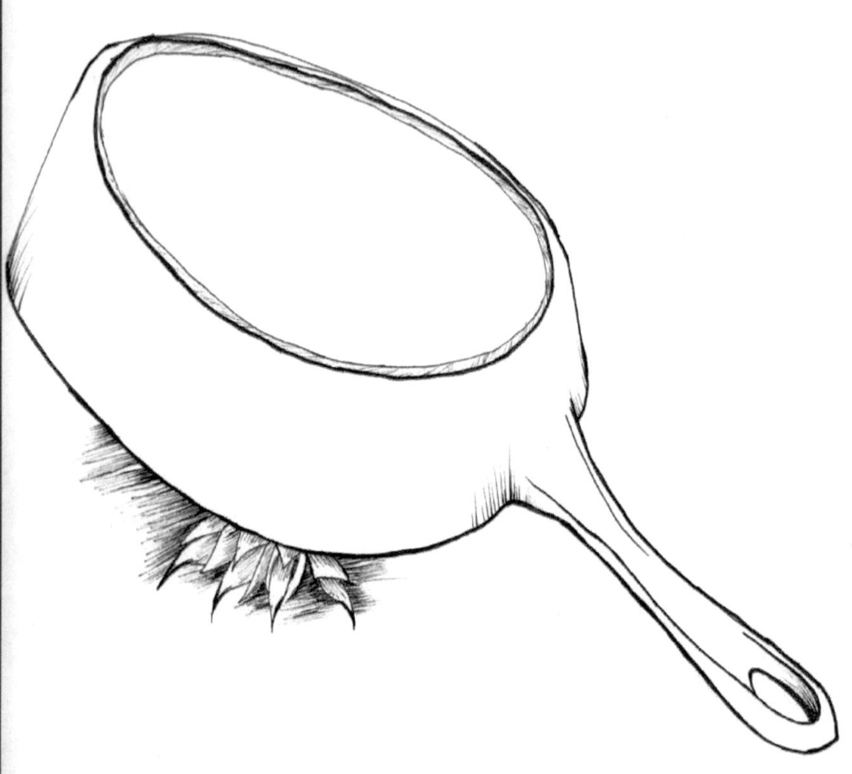

Although you'd like to believe you could hold the boys off with your throwing skills, you've never actually thrown anything before. On the other hand, you've got long, fast legs and so does Arti.

You let go of the crate and drop to the floor beside the other dragon with a thump. His green gem-eyes go wide.

The boys grin. Two of them, the ones who didn't throw their gloves, start pulling on their pairs.

"Now we're both in it!" Arti cries.

"Run!" you shout, and take off through the boys' legs, careening left and right to avoid contact. You need to be past them before they have their gloves on and are willing to touch you.

At first, Arti doesn't follow.

Although you want to, you can't wait for him. As you skitter past, the boys jump back. In the scramble, one of them knocks into a stack of crates. The top one rattles and tips, and then tumbles to the floor.

There's a massive crash, the shattering of glass, and something splatters your legs. Still not looking back, you scurry up the stairs and slam your shoulder into the door at the top. Thankfully, it swings on two-way hinges and the weight of your body is enough to shove it open.

You bolt through…and come to a skidding halt at the feet of the largest man you've ever seen. He glares down his spattered apron and stomps a foot onto your tail when you try to dart away.

Your chest buzzes and fizzles. Your defect does that sometimes, but even if it had zapped, it wouldn't have harmed him. His boots have thick soles.

"Are those my peaches splattered across your wings?"

The sweet smell of the peaches seems to accuse you. You're about to respond when Arti shoves through the door and skids to a stop too. The cook, for that's what he has to be, grabs a pot and tips it upside down over Arti's head. Then he sets a cast iron skillet over that to keep the dragon contained.

Satisfied, he stoops to pick you up.

"Don't touch me!"

No human has ever listened to your warning before. You stare at the cook, surprised, when he stops with his hand a mere inch from your back.

"Why?" he asks, suspiciously.

It's a moment before you can respond.

He's actually talking to you!

"I can't help shocking people," you cringe as you finally admit your defect.

"Really?" He eyes you. "Why are you covered in my peaches?"

His voice booms and you cower. Pointing a claw back at the basement, you squeak, "Street boys."

His face goes red. "Again!" His boot moves off your tail. "Stay put!" he orders and then stomps down the stairs.

A moment later, he reappears with the three boys hurrying in front of him. He shoves them out the door and shouts, "And stay out!"

It's only when he turns back that you realize that you might have escaped while he was occupied. But it's too late now. He plants his hands on his hips and stares at you, taking in the mess of peach juice now splattering his floor and the nearby upturned pot. It rattles but the skillet on top doesn't budge.

"Does heat bother you?" he asks.

Confused, you tilt your head. "No," you answer. "I don't think so."

"Can that one peel carrots?" He points at the skillet.

"Probably." You have no idea, but you're not going to admit that when he still looks so angry.

"Good," the cook says. "Stir that pot for me tonight and I'll call my peaches even. Have that one peel those carrots. Same deal."

He stomps away before you can respond.

You shove the skillet off Arti's pot and free him, explaining the situation.

"Really?" he says. "I can peel carrots!"

It's not your intention to stay with the cook and Arti, but when you lay down beside the cookfire that night, its warmth seeps into your metal scales and you experience the first full night's sleep of your life. One day slips into two, then they meld into three and before you know it, it's been a week and then a month.

You're still covered in soot, but now it's from stirring the cookpot. Arti's still clumsy, but he doesn't need his tail to peel and chop veggies.

One day you realize, life's good. You like the heat of the cookfire, the smell of simmering beef stew, and the laughter of the cook and Arti. They know not to touch you and that works out fine too. At night, you and Arti sleep beside the warm hearth and if, by chance, a rat wanders near the larder, the zap from your tail seems welcome too.

The End

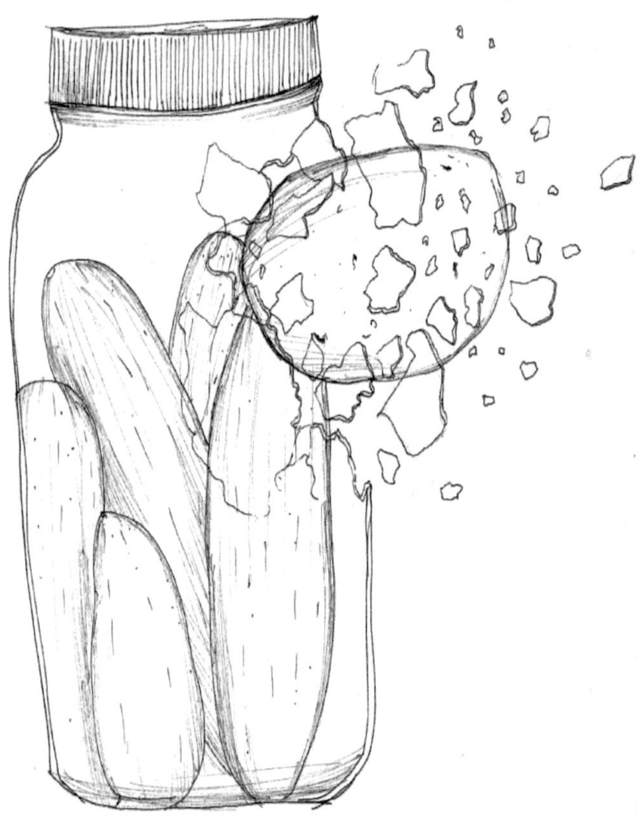

You're a fast runner and if you saw an opening between the boys' legs, you'd make a dash for it, but as you consider your options, the boys spread out and any openings quickly disappear.

You scramble on top of the crates and grab a potato. Its solid weight feels perfect as you lob it at the nearest boy. Turns out, although you've never thrown anything before, you have a strong arm.

He ducks and the potato smashes into the shelf behind him. Jars shatter. Liquid explodes. Dark splatters appear all over the boy and suddenly the basement smells like vinegar and pickles.

You're so surprised you almost forget to throw the next potato. Movement pulls you from your shock and you toss with barely a look at the boy approaching from the other side.

He tries to catch it, fumbles, and hits the stack of crates next to him with his elbow. There's a crack as the wood splinters. A bunch of carrots spill out of the new hole.

The crate you stand on wobbles, and you chance a peek to see Arti climbing toward you.

Good. He guessed your intention.

You throw another potato.

The third boy catches it but misses the second one you throw next. It smacks him between the eyes before thumping to the floor.

Your whoop of excitement dies in your throat as a shaft of light suddenly appears from the doorway across the basement. A set of stairs leads upward to the door and all you see at first is the brilliant light and two massive feet. Then the largest man you've ever seen enters the basement with a lantern in hand.

"What's the ruckus?!"

The boys freeze. The lantern glints off their suddenly terrified expressions. One makes to bolt for the window they used earlier but the man booms out, "Don't even try it," and he freezes again.

The man swings his lantern around, casting light across the dripping shelves, the glitter of shattered glass, the pile of rolling carrots, and the five unwelcome occupants.

He picks up a dripping potato and zeroes in on you and the potato you still hold in your paw. You drop it back into the crate with a soft thump.

A shudder starts to vibrate the wood under your feet, and you realize Arti is shaking where he still hangs off the side.

"You three," the man points at the boys. "There's a bucket and rags in that corner. Clean this up or I'll call the Watch on you."

The boys sag but head for the corner.

"You two," he points at you and Arti, "get out."

"But sir—" one of the boys starts to protest. He cuts off when the man spins toward him.

Arti finishes crawling to the top of the crates and you both slip through the bars of the window while the man is dealing with the street boys. It's a tighter fit than you expected it'd be and the bars screech as they scrape against your chest plates.

Arti moves to help.

"No, don't!"

He backs away and you finish wriggling through. Once out, you pause on the night-darkened street. You've no idea what to do now.

"Hey," Arti says. "I know a place we can find some parts. With your help, I might be able to put a tail together." He pauses and looks down at his feet. "But it's a long way from here and I can't fly. You okay with waddling there?"

You grin, your rusted gears creaking, "Got nothing else to do," you say, "but it'll be tricky to help you since I zap people when they touch me."

Arti tilts his head, and you notice he's missing a gear near his jaw. "The boys thought leather would insulate them. Maybe we can find some leather?"

You're reminded of the scraps that fell out of the Maker's dumpster when he tossed you.

"That could work. I think I know just the place to find some too."

And so, you start off down the street, waddling toward the Maker's shop and then the junkyard beyond.

The End

Acknowledgments

There's something incredibly fun about the *Discarded Dragons/Zap Dragon* world. Thank you to everyone who encouraged me to write more after *Discarded Dragons* came out!

For some reason, the acknowledgements are sometimes the hardest part for me to write. Words just don't fully express my gratitude for the amazing people who help me do what I love, but I'll give it another try.

Thank you to my beta readers, Nate, Mollie, Leslie, Nick, Mom and Dad, Myles, and David. You help me see my blind spots, help the characters come alive, and help the world of magic seem seamless. Few know the amount of work that goes into making a book but each of you willingly and enthusiastically make that work easier.

After the beta readers do their part, Darren Thornberry helps take the manuscript that last mile to polished book. Without his editing, I'd have some very embarrassing oopses. It's a blessing to work with him. Thank you, Darren, for your enthusiasm and wonderful work ethic.

By now, if you're familiar with my work, you're familiar with Justin Allen's. He's done all but one of my covers and a number of my illustrations. For *Zap Dragon*, Justin again took my very vague idea of a cover and turned it into an amazing reality. I can't thank you enough for your patience and vision.

Speaking of artwork, I couldn't not ask Esther Rohman to illustrate *Zap Dragon* after her incredible work on *Discarded Dragons*. Her artwork has just the right tone and feel for this world. Thank you, Esther, for sharing your gift to make this book what it is.

As always, I have to give my husband, Nate, his own shout out. It's no exaggeration to say I wouldn't be writing without his unwavering support. There's a verse in Ecclesiastes that says a threefold cord is not easily being broken. My husband helps keep me strong. Helps me strive for my dreams even when I waver.

And last, but far from least, thank you, Readers, for giving my writing a chance. I love hearing about how the Adventures bring a slice of joy to readers. You make the work worthwhile.

Other Books by Jennifer M Zeiger

Adventure Books

Discarded Dragons

Explore all 12 possible endings while getting to be a steam punk metal dragon.

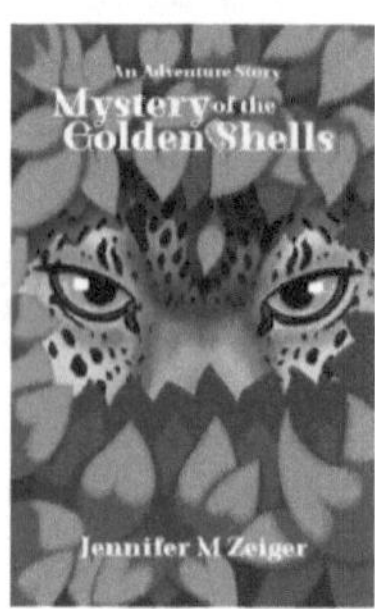

Mystery of the Golden Shells

Explore all 10 possible endings in this mystery who-done-it on an island with wild magic.

The Adventure

Explore all 26 possible endings in this sampler with 3 distinct stories. Investigate the myth on Moonrise Mountain, explore a dangerous cave system for treasure, and compete in a medieval style tournament.

Hidden Mythics Novels

Quaking Soul

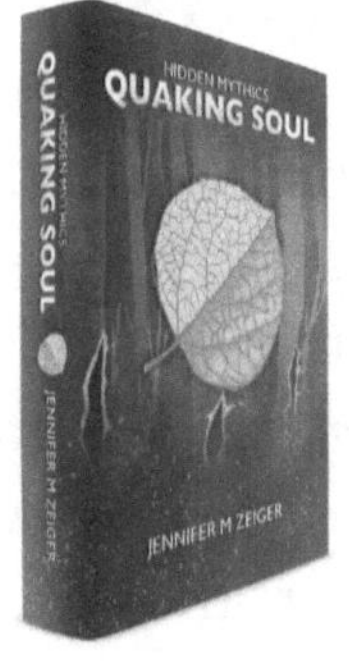

This is it. This is Na'rina's chance to prove to her mother and the Dryad Council she can navigate the mythic and human worlds. With night hanging over the city, all she needs to do is sneak in unseen, attend a mythic meeting, and report back.

Na'rina is a young Drydanda, destined to be Queen of the Dryads, or tree nymphs. Her world—fauns, nymphs, dwarves—hides in plain sight from the more populated human world. As long as they remain myth, they remain safe.

He's come to warn them but he's a wer-im, a werecat, who was banished centuries ago with the rest of his species for burning the dryad's trees. But humans captured his leader and dozens of other mythical creatures as well. If the mythic world is to survive, he must forge alliances.

When Na'rina's mother goes missing, she finds the violent, banished wer-im her only allies. She soon realizes that everything she's been taught about leadership appears to be wrong.

Who can Na'rina trust? As she quickly discovers, the fate of the mythical world rests on her decisions.

Jennifer M Zeiger grew up in the Rocky Mountains of Colorado and now lives in South Carolina with her husband, Nate.

She blogs multi-ending adventure stories and has now turned six of those into books—Three in *The Adventure* and now three stand-alones: *Discarded Dragons*, *Mystery of the Golden Shells*, and *Zap Dragon*. She also writes fantasy novels. Check out *Quaking Soul* for the first installment in the Hidden Mythics series.

jenniferzeiger.com

Hello Dear Reader,

Thank you so much for reading *Zap Dragon!* I hope you enjoyed it. It is only because of people like you, people who give my writing a chance, that I'm able to do what I truly love.

If you enjoyed this book and would like to help, then please consider leaving a review on Amazon, Goodreads, or anywhere else readers visit. Word of mouth is a huge part of how well a book sells, so if you leave one, you are directly helping me continue this journey as a full-time writer. Thank you in advance to anyone who does. It means the world to me!

Many Blessings,

Jennifer

Amazon